THE

HORRORS

OF

OAKENDALE

ABBEY.

A ROMANCE

BY

MRS. CARVER

THE HORRORS OF
OAKENDALE ABBEY.

Mrs. Carver

Introduction and Notes by Curt Herr

ZITTAW PRESS

Zittaw Press: *The Horrors of Oakendale Abbey* first printed in Great Britain by
Minerva Press in 1797.

ISBN: 0-9767212-8-7

Zittaw Press welcomes comments and suggestions regarding any aspect of this
reproduction—please contact us at customerservice@zittaw.com.

www.zittaw.com

To the Coffin Room,
The Crawl-Spaces of Crosspatch,
and to Haley ... who wore crosses.

they describe the elements contained within the plot and narrative structure of the novel itself. Male Gothic fiction tends to focus on the desire to break into—to penetrate an intimate space. Erotic in tone, perverse in nature, plots of Male Gothic focus on the destruction of social taboos and codes of security such as religion, family and social institutions. Stressing violence and supernatural elements, ghosts, demons, sexual predators and the walking dead are frequent tropes of this genre. Supernatural events are rarely explained with rationality, for Male Gothic fiction is a reaction against the logical and rational order of the universe. Evil exists because—well—evil *exists*.

Female Gothic fiction however, examines the metaphor behind the violence—the silent voice of women locked within the world of terrifying men. Avoiding sensationalistic plots like those of Walpole's *The Castle of Otranto* and Lewis' *The Monk*, writers of Female Gothic fiction focus on the female's attempt to break free from patriarchally enforced prisons. Supernatural elements are used—but are always explained with logical rationale. The ghosts and demons of Male Gothic fiction do not exist—but evil men do. Emily St. Aubert of Radcliff's *Mysteries of Udolpho* spends about 1/3 of the lengthy novel attempting to escape from the prison/castle where she has been trapped. Her most frightening experience occurs when she discovers an unknown corpse behind a curtain—only to discover chapters later that the corpse is simply a wax dummy and not a threat at all. The fear of terror and paranoid heroines is healed by logical explanations and the restoration of rational order.

Additionally, women in this genre become trapped in male interiors and consequently, transform themselves into either passive prisoners or active archaeologists. Those who succumb to the former usually die at the hands of villainous men, while those who become the latter discover they are capable of great transformations—in themselves and in others. Many of these women explore their castle/abbey/prison with great energy. They search for the weak places in the walls, floors, attics, (and in the hearts of men) in their attempt to not merely escape, but more significantly, to discover freedom. Bronte's Jane Eyre in Thornfield Hall, Roseline in Bonhote's *Bungay Castle*, Mina in Stoker's *Dracula*, and Eleanor in Jackson's *The Haunting of Hill House* all discover ways of escaping their socially imposed bonds—some more successfully than others. Jane Eyre tames the Gothic hero, yet Eleanor Vance succumbs to Hill House's psychological terror and destroys herself. Thus, a reprint of Mrs. Carver's *The Horrors of Oakendale Abbey* is an important find in the crypt of lost Gothic novels, for Carver breaks all these rules and does so with staggering results. If Gothic novels are based upon the rejection of a logical ordered social structure, Oakendale Abbey is the Empire State of haunted houses.

Oakendale Abbey: Staring Into the Casket

The basic requirements of Female Gothic are certainly present in Carver's rediscovered novel: a lonely heroine trapped in a crumbling, monstrously large Abbey, an evil patriarch with lusty designs upon her body, and plenty of supernatural hauntings—or so we perceive. However, Carver is a rare wordsmith in Female Gothic fiction for she is not a polite or a kind writer; she does not shy away from disturbing topics or grotesque imagery like many of her contemporaries. She is direct, confrontational, disgustingly descriptive, and quite violent—all male elements. Due to these threatening components, she is not easy on her heroines. She frequently forces women to revisit scenes of exquisite horror, wrenching the protective veil from their eyes with exquisite force. She directs her frightened heroines to stare at death in all of its gruesome grandeur—and not look away. Akin to contemporary slasher flicks, these women intimately confront horrifying scenes of rotting corpses and hacked up body parts. In Carver's fiction, there is an extreme focus on physical putrescence found in death, decay, and believe it or not, misused corpses, (hardly the stuff of Radcliff's *Mysteries of Udolpho* or Austin's Gothic satire, *Northanger Abbey*). In her epistolary novel *The Old Woman*, written in 1800, Carver's character, Mrs Clifford, describes a friend's drowned corpse in exquisitely precise detail. I include the entire passage to demonstrate Carver's emphasis upon minutely detailed grotesque imagery:

> According to my directions, Lucy had ordered the coffin to be so slightly screwed, that the lid was easily again taken off.—There is a something in the contemplation of a dead body, even under the most uninteresting circumstances, which is awful in the extreme. I confess, when I entered the room, I shuddered, not with horror or fear, but an indescribable sensation seemed to overpower me, and it was some moments before I could recover myself sufficiently to approach the coffin, and when I beheld the mangled features of our dear departed Julia, I could not avoid uttering a shriek of terror. Lucy supported and encouraged me to examine the features of her beloved mistress; the

frequent sight having rendered her less shocked at the contemplation of an object so dreadful.

> The body was dressed exactly as it was found in the water, that is, the remains of the dress, for it was partly torn to pieces, and the face so entirely mutilated, that it must be impossible to ascertain from that whether or not it was really Julia. The size and shape corresponded with her's, and the hair is the same colour, but upon examining the hands, I think they appeared larger, and not so beautifully formed as were Julia's; but this might be accounted for by having been so long under the water, and being swoln (sic). Her stockings and the remains of her linen were marked J.S. and Lucy says, she could swear to the work being her's. The gown was the very one in which she had dressed her on the day she was missing. These are proofs strong enough of the body's being no other than that of our unhappy friend, ... [A]s to the face, as I said before, it is so entirely mutilated, that no trace of feature or countenance could possibly be discovered. (Carver *The Old Woman* Vol II, Letter XVI)

The ripped dress, the face mangled beyond recognition, the swollen, long submerged body—Carver focuses our attention upon the body's inability to withstand death and its consequences. Death is not pretty in Carver's world. This is not a romanticized image of grace and dignity in death—it is a horrific confrontation of one of our most personal fears: our inability to control what occurs to our bodies after death. This is the ultimate loss of self control. Death is described as an ugly, horrific invasion of the most intimate manner—a horrifying thought—and a significant part of the novel you are currently holding in

14

your hands. The description of Julia's corpse is perversely intimate. The coffin must be unscrewed—indeed, invaded—to allow the women to view the corpse. Extreme effort is taken to look upon the hideous package inside. Knowing she drowned, knowing the body was long submerged, Mrs. Clifford still desires to consciously confront what she knows will be a horrific image. To make this matter even more ghastly, Carver's epistolary narrative form forces the narrator to not only view the body, but also to write about it as well—forever searing the descriptive words in her own memory—and all who read the letter.

Carver's emphasis upon forced confrontation with ghastly elements is especially evident in *The Horrors of Oakendale Abbey*. Her hapless yet unusually resilient heroine, Laura, is trapped in the decayed, coffin-like Abbey—a Gothic maze of mythic ghost stories, urban legends, and actual walking corpses. Local legends describe murderous rooms that drip with blood, a ghostly female figure with a slit throat silently peers from behind cobwebbed windows, and all who go near the Abbey will be captured to live with the violent and vengeful ghosts—horrifying consequences indeed. However, Carver does not allow her heroine to run away from terrifying events for long—nor does she bestow upon her female characters the kind gift of fainting. Instead, Carver asks her heroines to consciously experience horror with no recourse of escape. Rather than simply running away and passively waiting for a male to rescue them, they gaze upon rotting corpses and walking cadavers with wide-eyed terror. Furthermore, not satisfied with a single viewing, Carver doubles the horror by forcing her heroines to return to the scene of terror. They physically return to the open coffin, the crypt, or the bloody chamber (...and we all know this is a no-brainer). Sometimes they repeat the story to someone—telling the terrified listener of their ghastly encounter. Although this may seem like cruel repetition, Carver makes silent experience vocal. She gives a voice to their terror while accentuating the physical horror they experienced. More importantly, it creates a community of shared experience—an empowering element. Through repeating the actions of their experience—either physically or vocally—they are more prepared to internalize the details and consume the terror in hopes of understanding the event on a more intellectual level. It is the isolated individual, the passive sufferer who refuses to understand experience, who fails in many Gothic plots. *The Monk's* Antonia intuitively knows that evil may befall her— yet she isolates herself and does not intellectually understand her predicament—forced codes of religion and her adherence to the socially prescribed value of virginity has made her the perfect passive victim. Carver, however, does not allow her heroines to succumb to this tragic end. Through exploring their prisons and challenging their abilities to confront the terrible, her heroines emerge triumphant—though somewhat bruised from the experience. Like heroes of mythic classic tales, they realize that understanding comes from experiencing. They have gained qualities that subconsciously existed within their silent psyches, yet were never needed or used due to their previously passive existence.

Oakendale Abbey: The Jails of Jealous Men
Enriching her exploration of the effects of terror, Carver also examines the psychological roots in the quest for power and

control through the use of perverse desires and corrupt impulses. Central to Gothic novels is the theme of power—the desire of gaining it or the fear of losing it. Power can appear in many diverse forms: sexual power (*The Monk),* power over women (*The Mysteries of Udolpho*), power over legacy and lineage (*The Castle of Otranto),* power over a populous (*Dracula* and *The Beetle*) or power over the self (Anne Rice's Vampire Chronicles, Jackson's *The Haunting of Hill House*, King's *The Shining*). Carver, however, goes beyond these surface desires for power. She reaches back to the beginning of time and examines the most basic desire for power: male jealously of the birth process. Predating Shelley's Victor Frankenstein by 20 years, Carver examines and uncovers of the perverse male desire to control and replicate the birth process for their own selfish needs.

First, Carver makes connections between the male and the coffin/womb-like Abbey. Like Poe's *House of Usher*, the house and the family name are synonymous. Lord Oakendale and his Abbey are representative of each other even though he has never travelled inside the very structure he owns. They are both monstrous creations who desire to create, control, and destroy life. Additionally, they are capable of consuming the very life they create. For example, Lord Oakendale and his wife have no children. Completely barren, they are not intimate with each other nor do they enjoy each other's company. A pre-arranged marriage for financial gain—both partners are bitter and distanced. When Lord Oakendale sees the much younger Laura walking along the beach- he instantly consumes her. He claims her as his future wife/daughter/sex-toy. Because she refuses his advances, Lord Oakendale punishes her. He locks Laura away in his ghastly Abbey hoping solitude in the horrific environment will make him more attractive in her eyes. Unlike *Otranto's* Manfred, Lord Oakendale does not desire children and is not concerned about the legacy of his family name. His desires are purely centered on physical lust and consuming sexual dominance. Viewing sexual desire as a selfish act with no better purpose (i.e. childbirth), Lord Oakendale is purely motivated by personal sexual gratification. His desire is in direct opposition with the birthing process. It is an act of de-creation rather than creation—a desire to consume, not to consummate. Through symbolic ingesting, he is able to completely control the item devoured and use it for his own benefits. A 16th century German woodcut by Hans Weiditz illustrates this perverse male desire with graphic results. (See illustration) Der Kinderfresser, or The Child-Eater is a folk-lore father-like figure who devours children. The woodcut depicts an older, ogre-like man with wild hair and a huge mouth—a grandfather gone wrong. Horrified screaming children spill from his arms and highly suggestive yonic-like purse as he pops them into his mouth with a ferocious appetite. The children react with grotesquely precise detail as they weep, moan and even defecate in fear. Similar to Carver's unflinching detail, none of them looks away from the approaching horror- none of them close their eyes to shield the advancing jaws of the consuming father (except for one lucky infant- and he is dead, dangling from the father's belt like a perversely discarded decoration). The veil of protective unconsciousness wrenched from their eyes, they see with terrified consciousness the doom that awaits them. Lord Oakendale repeats the atrocities of The Child-Eater in his desires and actions. In his ambition for absolute domination over

Laura's life and body, he devourers her hoping she'll be reborn into the child/lover/object he desires. Like the children dangling from The Child Eater's belt, she consciously realizes his

horrifying plan while staring into the widening jaws of the consuming father: the most perverse father of them all.

Consequently, Carver's Abbey becomes the horrifying symbol of the dead male womb. It is both the ultimate female space (a nunnery) and the reversal of that very space—a womb of disintegration and de-creation. A large and sprawling gothic mansion, the Abbey's original intention was to house nuns—

women focused upon life everlasting and ironically, a celibate community. By the time Carver's novel opens, the Abbey has not been inhabited for decades. It is a dead space, barren, and completely void of creating new life. Taken over by Resurrection Men, freshly unearthed corpses are brought into this terrible womb, not for healing, but for dissecting—ripping apart, thus reversing the life process. Lord Oakendale uses it in much the same fashion. It is a prison for isolating women who refuse the advances of powerful men. He also reverses this theme of barren space, for like a perverse mother, he is expecting. Placing Laura with in this womb/tomb, he symbolically penetrates the abbey's walls with phallic aggression and like Shelley's Victor Frankenstein, he expects a hideous re-birth. He expects Laura to be reborn into a silent, passive female who will cling to him alone. Lord Oakendale and his Abbey replicates both the hideous Child-Eater/father and the perverse mother who gives birth while taking life. Destroying the paternal and societal concept of protection, it is the desire of absolute control over bodies and fates which infects the novel through the very end.

With in the walls of her monstrous Abbey, Carver intimately illustrates horrors which haunt the reader long after putting her book down. If the 18th century can be characterized as a time which stressed rationality, logic, and the primacy of reason over romantic notions, Carver's Oakendale Abbey accentuates the reverse with drastic effects. Like the cold grasp of a dead hand, her images and themes refuse to let go. They pull us into the dark grave to lie with the clutching corpse. According to *The Horrors of Oakendale Abbey*, we have no escape from the terrors that await us behind the closed door or beyond the darkened grave.

Shattering the concept of Female Gothic fiction, Carver's supernatural hauntings are indeed explained—but the explanation terrifies us even more. In Carver's world, horrific men do indeed exist and we have no control over them. The good suffer terribly, and the bad are never punished. Thus, rather than healing the terrors with her novel's conclusion, she creates an abundance of anxiety she chooses not to heal. We can be ripped from our innocent homes and decapitated upon the French guillotine—only to have our heads returned, staked on the iron fence we ironically thought protected us. We have no control over the designs and desires of sexual predators—we are victims lost in a world of Lord Oakendales ready to be mysteriously whisked away at any moment. Even the release of death brings anxiety for we can not control our bodies after burial. They are free to be dug up, harvested from the earth to be studied and dismantled by the cold staring eyes of unscrupulous men.

As her name implies, Carver wields a literary butcher's knife. She hacks to death the prescribed, predetermined plot structures of 18th century Gothic and creates a monster of contemporary anxieties and insecurities. Elements of romance, confidence, resolution, and happily-ever-after are hacked off and tossed aside to decompose on a filthy mulch pile of abandoned literary tropes. They have no place in Carver's Gothic. They would satisfy the reader and reassure us that the world can return to normal...it can't. Hideously wrenching the veil from her reader's eyes, Carver demonstrates the most hideous lesson of them all: terror is real.

A Note on the Text

Although originally published in 1797 by Great Britain's Minerva Press, this edition of *The Horrors of Oakendale Abbey* is set from the first American edition of 1799 printed and sold by John Harrisson of New York. Most of Carver's original spelling and punctuation have been retained. I have made the following corrections:

Page Breaks—The original text is written without chapters or page breaks. I have added small chapter breaks between some of the plot lines for ease and clarity of reading.

I cleared up a confusing pronoun reference and publication error. Page 35. "Two years after the death of the late Earl, he found himself..." I replaced 'he' with 'Robert.'

Page 36. "Meantime, Robert returned from the field of battle..." I have replaced 'Robert' with "William'- William is the kind heroic brother who goes off to war, not Robert.

The
Horrors of Oakendale Abbey.

In the gloomy month of November, when the mountains in Cumberland were almost concealed by the heavy black clouds which hung below their tops, and a thick dripping rain scarcely left the few scattered cottages of Oakendale discernable, the peasants were all retired to their habitations; and through this thick atmosphere the stately ruins of the antient Abbey appeared like a black mass of immense length, and could only be distinguished as a building, by the glimmering twinkling of the small panes of glass from some of the many windows which were dispersed without uniformity, in this gloomy structure.

The church clock had struck five, when a loud knocking at the cottage of Aaron Giles (who was intrusted with the keys of the Abbey) roused him from a slumber to which the labours of the day, and the stillness of the evening, had composed him, and caused a strange alarm to the rest of his family, consisting of a notable

Dame, now seated at the spinning wheel, a beautiful girl about fourteen years of age, and two stout boys, who were quietly eating a piece of brown bread.—"Lord," cried the wife and daughter, both in the same breath, "what can that be?—Don't open the door, father," said the girl, "for fear it should be one of the spirits from the Abbey."

The repeated knocking sufficiently awakened Aaron, terrified the rest of the family, and a voice demanded instant admittance.

Aaron, half bold and half afraid, regardless of the entreaties of those about him, ventured to undraw the bolt, and ask "Who was there?"

"You must open the door," replied a quick voice, "and deliver to me the keys of the Abbey."[1]

Aaron, who had by this time opened the door sufficiently to distinguish a servant well mounted with a livery great coat on, entirely lost all fear and replied, "The keys of the Abbey! why, nobody would venture there at this time of night what can they be wanted for?"

---

[1] Keys are highly symbolic items that can represent power, authority, and agency. To hold a key can represent the bearer has been inducted to the world beyond the locked door or gate—is knowledgeable and experienced where the keyless others are naive and lacking. In the classic fairy tales which Mrs Carver was certainly aware of, keys represent a mystery to be solved, a task which needs completion, or at their most extreme, a life-risking test of courage and strength. Most notably used in Blue Beard or Angel Carter's revision 'The Bloody Chamber'.

"For a lady," replied the servant, "who will be here within two hours, and you must go with me; and your wife must come also, to make a fire, and get things in a little order and comfort for my Lady."

"Order and comfort for my Lady!" said Aaron (holding the door fast in his hand) "I am sure there is no order or comfort to be had there."

"No, no," said his wife, advancing fearfully; nobody don't like to go there in day-time, much more when it is dark; and master must not deliver the keys to any but my Lord himself, or to Master Acre, the steward."

"Prithee, give me the keys," said the servant "and keep me here no longer; for I have orders, both from my Lord and Mr. Acre, and to receive them; so do not trifle, for no time is to be lost."

Aaron, scratching his head, knew not what to do; but told the man "he had better come in a bit; as for going to the Abbey, it was sooner said than done.—Why," said he, "you do not know what you ask; we might be carried away, and never heard on any more. I never ventures in there without two or three as stout as myself with me, and then we be just frightened out of our lives."

"Never fear," replied the footman, who had by this time dismounted, and was advancing into the house; at the same time taking a pistol from his pocket, which he held in a menacing manner, saying, "What the devil are you afraid of? Why, I will engage to blow up all the ghosts in the country, if you will give me a draught of something to drink, for I am devilish dry."

The good woman, trembling replied, "She would give him some cider, provided he would put up the pistol, and not be blasphemous; and the poor little girl, who with her brothers had fled to the further corner of the room, on seeing the pistol which he still held in his hand, advanced, fell upon her knees, and begged him not to kill them, for none of them had done any harm.

The beauty and innocence of this girl softened the valiant boastings of the footman; and he instantly returned the pistol to his pocket, saying, "No, my pretty dear, I have no intention to hurt you."[2]

During this time, Aaron was reading a letter the servant had given him, which contained an order from Lord Oakendale, for his instantly preparing the Abbey for the reception of a Lady, who would be there on that very evening. Aaron, terrified at the idea of the undertaking, and yet seeing the necessity of his obedience, instantly summoned two of his neighbours, who, together with the footman and himself, prepared

---

[2] Carver accentuates a long history of the power of beauty and innocence with this moment. Like many young and innocent women, this young girl is unaware of the power contained in her beauty and its ability to transform the viewer. Like Belle in "Beauty and the Beast," beauty transforms the beast-like visitor into a kind and reassuring gentleman. Although Mrs Carver relies heavily upon this motif throughout her Gothic novel, she does not simply repeat the established pattern- she destroys it with a vengeance. It takes more than beauty and innocence to destroy the nightmare of Oakendale Abbey.

peasants, by asking them "if they resided there, and if they could assure her there were no other persons in the Abbey?"

"Lack-a-day!" said Dame Giles, "we be none on us to stay here; we only comed to make a fire, and get a little ready for your Ladyship and I'm afeared as how you'll find it very lonesome being in this dismal place by yourselves."

"Not at all," returned the Lady, "provided I am unmolested."

Dame Giles looked grave, and thought within herself that was not certain; but she would not say any thing that might occasion fears of evil spirits to this young Lady, who seemed entirely free from any such apprehensions, and for whom she conceived the highest veneration, mixed with the tenderest pity, for being destined to an abode in her opinion, so dangerous.

When she attended her to the apartment where the bed was, and apologized for the coarseness of the sheets and bed clothes, which had been furnished from her cottage, the Lady gave a look of surprise at the antiquity of the bed, and the gloomy magnificence of the room, which was large, with an immense fire-place; a long gothic window on the right, on the small pains of which were painted serpents, dragons, and such unmeaning and hideous monsters;[7] a smaller window was placed in a corner on the left, and the ragged tapestry represented still more horrible figures, all of which waved in life-like movements as the air (admitted by the door) fanned the loose hanging on which they were represented.—She surveyed in silence the dismal appearance of the whole; and then said (with a sigh) "I shall find no fault I believe; but shall probably sleep quieter then I have done for many nights past, in pleasanter rooms, and beds that seemed better calculated for repose."[8]

The person who had come with her seemed to survey every thing with a countenance of horror, and an expression of fear; and, turning to the young Lady, said "My dear Madam, is it possible that we can stay in this melancholy place alone? Why, I never saw any thing half so dismal; I shall not, I am sure, close my eyes in that frightful bed. Cannot you," addressing Dame Giles, "stay with us to night?"

---

[7] In Eastern cultures, dragons are celestial symbols- often representing happiness as they are capable of creating the potion which ensures everlasting life. However, in Western cultures, dragons have been used to symbolize evil guards and satanic sentries. Often demonic and vicious, they guard the desired riches of immortality.

[8] Clearly setting her apart from the lower classes who surround her, Laura does not give in to emotional and subjective responses to the frightening images before her. Another example of Laura's strength, Carver stresses Laura's common sense and no nonsense approach to her terrible situation.

"No," replied the other; "I cannot, at the same time thinking she would not, for all the world."

The young Lady, whose name was Laura, said to her companion, "Why, surely you are not afraid of ghosts! and at present I see nothing else to fear here; but, addressing herself to the daughter of Dame Giles, who was close to her mother, she said, "Perhaps you will stay with us, my little maid; and when there are three of us we cannot be afraid."

"No," said Peggy, "I wo nut stay."

"Well, as you please," said Laura; "and as I am much fatigued, I will not detain you any longer."

Dame Giles replenished the fire, left them a sufficient number of lights, and departed, promising to come there early in the morning to prepare their breakfasts. Meantime the footman had been giving orders to Aaron to go to the next market town, and provide them with every necessary for their accommodation. He then delivered a letter into the hands of Laura, and then respectfully withdrew. He returned to the cottage with Aaron, and the other two men; where, mounting his horse, he rode away. The cottagers spent some time wondering at the strangeness of the adventure, and expressing their fears, lest the Ladies might be carried away by the evil spirits which were said to haunt the Abbey.

Having left Laura and her companion in the Abbey, and the inhabitants of Oakendale quietly taking their repose, it may be necessary to give the reader some account of the family to whom the Abbey belonged, and how Laura came to be its present inhabitant.

The present Lord Oakendale had succeeded in a lenial descent to the Earldom and estates of Oakendale. His great-grandfather was the only one that the eldest inhabitant of the village could remember, and that memory was impressed by wicked and atrocious deeds, said to have been committed by this old Earl, since which time it had never been inhabited more than for a few days, when the present Lord's father brought down a beautiful woman, who was his wife, and mother to the present Earl; her picture was said to be still in one of the rooms.

It was currently reported, that various figures had been seen flitting about after twilight; ghastly visions had appeared, smeared with blood; and the ghost of a lady, who was supposed to have been murdered in one of the rooms, was usually seen after it was dark looking through the windows, with streams of blood running from her throat.[9] Tales of this nature had filled the

---

[9] This ghostly figure is an important metaphor Carver's novel. A female featuring a slit throat is a violent reminder of the history of voiceless women—or the punishment bestowed upon vocal females. From Antigone and Cordelia, to the fairy tales of the Brothers' Grimm, (*The Six Swans, Blue Beard*), and Anderson's *The Little Mermaid*, the female

minds of the simple villagers with dreadful apprehensions; but what had given more reasonable colour and strength to these fears were, two circumstances, which had happened within only a twelve-month of each other; one was, that of a young gentleman's never being heard of after going to explore the Abbey; the other, of another gentleman's endeavouring to sleep there, who was so extremely terrified by noises, howlings and phantoms, that, although a determined and resolute man, he was obliged to relinquish the design, and to pass the remainder of the night with one of the villagers in a cottage.

Lord Oakendale, the present Earl, had never seen the Abbey; he had no doubt heard the reports, but, being a very dissipated man, he gave no heed to them, much less had any desire to have them investigated. He was the eldest of two brothers, who were the only surviving sons of a numerous progeny. Their dispositions, manners, persons and sentiments, were, from their earliest childhood, so totally opposite, that not the most distant similarity could ever be discovered. Robert, the elder, who was the present Earl, was haughty, imperious, vindictive, vain and artful; and, if any spring of latent virtue arose in his heart, it was suppressed and overpowered by these vices. His person was far superior to this mind; for there, indeed, the graces shone forth

---

voice has a long history of enforced silence and the struggle to regain vocalized experience.

with conspicuous lustre. He was tall, well proportioned, and of a bold and manly countenance. His brother William, though less in stature, was equally well made, and had the most engaging and attractive features. An expressive countenance displayed a mind fraught with every manly virtue that could adorn a Christian and a soldier. At a very early age he entered the army, and distinguished himself in the service of his country by more than one noble and gallant action; during which time his brother was leading a life, not only of inactivity, but of unlimited debauchery of every kind. Two years after the death of the late Earl, Robert found himself so embarrassed and his fortune so little equal to his expences, that he was under the necessity of repairing it by a marriage, in which love formed no part of the contract.

Miss Rainsford, the only child of Lord Westhaven, was the exact counterpart of her lover, if the appellation of lover could be given to one whose motives were guided by the desire of wealth or ambition; an union, founded upon such a basis, could be productive of nothing but discord; her fortune was perfectly convenient to him, and having secured that, he conceived a determined hatred to her. She followed her inclinations entirely; and, as they entertained a mutual indifference for each other, contempt and aversion soon followed.

Meantime William returned from the field of battle crowned with laurels and universal esteem. His many virtues called forth the envy and hatred of his brother, who could by no means bear to see himself so far eclipsed; and as this jealousy rankled in his heart, under the specious cover of love and regard he continued to undermine his advancement, and prevent his gaining that rank to which his merit so justly entitled him.— Unsuspicious, and judging of every heart by his own, William could not see through the hypocrisy of Lord Oakendale; and with a contented mind he patiently waited the dispensations of fortune. Thus looking forward with hope, with tender adieus to his brother, to whom he looked as his only relation and best friend, he embarked with his regiment for the East Indies. In the mean time Lord Oakendale continued his dissipated life, and, having no children, he had formed no cement of conjugal felicity. He had met with Laura in a very obscure part of South Wales, where he had been bathing the preceding autumn. He was wonderfully struck with her beauty, and altogether pleased with her manners. From the first moment he beheld her, he was determined to possess her person; and finding, upon acquaintance, that an uncommon delicacy and virtuous principle governed all her actions, he carefully concealed from her that he was a married man till he had learned her situation, and had, as he thought, made an interest in her affections, and secured every bar which might oppose his happiness. But, as her history will make a principle part of this work, we shall only at present inform our readers, that he had sent her to this dismal abode, under the idea that the horrors of the place, and the obscurity of the village, would sooner dispose a mind, like hers, to coincide with his base desires.

The letter the footman had left with her was from his Lordship, containing an apology for his having consigned her to so melancholy and rude a situation; assuring her that he should not intrude upon her retirement without her permissions, and concluding with his unalterable love and respect.

After Dame Giles and the other villagers had left Laura and she heard the gate of the Abbey locked upon her, a sound which terrified her more fearful companion, she opened and perused Lord Oakendale's letter, which having carelessly read, and gathering satisfaction from his promise of not coming there, she proposed going to bed, with the idea of enjoying a better night's rest than she had experienced for many of the past: but her companion wished to sit up, being, as she declared, afraid to consign herself to sleep in so dismal a room, and still more dismal looking bed. Laura, who entertained no fears of this nature, determined to undress herself, and seek that repose of which she stood in need; and Mary, her companion, being equally afraid to sit up, if Laura should go to sleep; therefore, however reluctantly, prepared to do the same. Laura, whose body was fatigued, and her mind totally divested of fear, soon fell into a profound sleep; but Mary, without ever having heard any tales concerning the Abbey gave way to the fancies she formed from its appearance; and a thousand apprehensions, of she knew not what, made her afraid to open her eyes, or to shut them, and by that means destroyed every idea of rest. She several times attempted to awake Laura, but found it impossible; she was therefore obliged to attend to the various noises which assailed her ear, without being able either to communicate her fears, or receive any comfort from her companion. The account she gave in the morning, was, that soon after she had been in bed, she plainly heard the sound of doors opening and shutting, and upon listening more attentively, she heard voices whispering, and footsteps at, or very near, the chamber door. All these relations, when repeated in the morning to Laura, she treated as idle chimeras of a fearful apprehension; declaring she had never in her life slept better, and that it was her fixed resolution to explore every part of the Abbey before the ensuing night.[10]

Dame Giles, attended by her daughter, arrived at the Abbey with their breakfasts; and pleased at finding them safe where she had left them, began making the fire, and moving about with more alacrity than she had done the

---

[10] Where all others fear and dread the Abbey, Laura desires to explore "every part" of it. She intuitively understands the need to explore her world.

preceding night; but gave little or no answer to the interrogatories of Mary concerning the Abbey, and who or what beings besides themselves were supposed to be the inhabitants of it.

Dame Giles said, "She knew of nobody being in it but themselves;" and, not willing to increase her fears, added, "That the passages were long and narrow, and the wind might whistle and draw through them like voices."

Laura, whose beautiful countenance, refreshed by sleep was animated with uncommon lustre, laughed at their conversation; again declaring her intention of taking a survey of the Abbey, as well as walking round the hills which seemed to surround it; the beauty of which she admired as she viewed them through the small casements of the windows.

The sun shone upon the tops of the hills, and its silver rays, which reflected upon the frosty turf with a dazzling whiteness, gave it a cheerful appearance.—"Tell me not," said she, "of voices and noises, here is nothing to create fear; hark, how the robin twitters his gentle note; and see how the frost glitters upon the verdure!¹¹ The winds only bespeak the wintry season, but nothing to inspire notions either of fear or dread. Ah! would fortune but smile upon me with the same benign aspect that the face of nature does, how little I should have to regret; and how well should I be pleased to remain all my

---

¹¹ Fresh, lush, flourishing vegetation. In great contrast with the sterile and decayed Abbey, the surroundings are fertile and healthy.

days in this sequestered retirement?[12] But, alas! no such happiness awaits me—a poor unprotected orphan, without a claim upon any human being, nothing but my own courage and virtue to guard me from the power of a villain! Ah me! my own reflections are the bitterest accompaniments of my solitude." During this soliloquy, which burst involuntarily from the oppressed heart of Laura, her two companions stood in mute attention, the one knowing or partly guessing, that she had just reason for her complaints, and the other staring at her without well understanding the meaning of her speech; which, being uttered in a pathetic voice, and in sentiments rather above her comprehension, induced her to entertain the idea of her being mad, and brought there for confinement; but when Laura turned her lovely face towards them, and the pearly tears chased each other down the fairest cheeks that nature ever formed, whilst her expressive eyes seemed to ask for pity's soothing voice, the gentler passions stole upon the heart of Dame Giles; she felt the most tender pity for the fair object before her, and, in a melting strain, she replied, "God help you, my poor young lady; sure no body would go to hurt so sweet a creature!" and looking at Mary, as if to

---

[12] Carver uses the Woman's Domestic Gothic theme throughout Oakendale Abbey. The female is victim trapped inside domestic walls that imprisons rather than protects her. This theme was most notably used in Radcliffe's *The Mysteries of Udolpho* (1794), Bronte's *Jane Eyre* (1847), and more recently in Carter's *The Magic Toyshop* (1967), and King's *The Shining* (1977).

gather some information from her concerning who and what they were, she continued, "Ah, ye must comfort one another, seeing, as I suppose, ye be sent here by our Lord's orders; and to be sure it is a melancholy place, and somehow I never thought as I could a been in it so long a time; but use makes perfect, and I bent so feared now as I was last night; and when I comes again to get your dinners, I thinks I shant be afeared at all."

"No," said Laura, "here is nothing to be afraid of; and I must desire you will give me the keys of all the rooms in the Abbey, that I may have the satisfaction of going over them."

"Why," said Dame Giles, "then here they be (at the same time giving her a bunch of rusty keys); but I think as how you had better be contended with this here room, and them that ye see below, for I believe the others be but dismal places, by all accounts; for I never seed them since I was a little un, and then went but a little way, and we was a good many on us."

"And what did you see?" said Mary, impatiently.

"Laws, Madam!" said Dame Giles, "I cant remember;" and so saying she hastened to leave them to make the search by themselves, lest they should have requested her to accompany them.

She was no sooner gone, and their breakfast over, than Laura, taking up the keys, said, "Come Mary, let us begin our survey. I promise myself great amusement from the employment, and I desire you will have no fears."

Mary looked as if she had rather have been excused; but casting her eyes round the room with a fearful kind of observation, the sun, which glimmering through the narrow panes of glass, diffused a cheering light, and rendered every object less gloomy than it had appeared the night before by only the light of the candles; she therefore consented to attend Laura, who led the way; and having left their chamber, she proceeded to her right along a low dark gallery, on the sides of which some doors opened into small rooms, most of them dark, and others admitting but a small portion of light, entirely without furniture except an old high backed chair, or the remains of an old stuffed couch.

The end of the gallery terminated in a narrow stone stair case, down which Laura, followed by her trembling companion, descended. When she came to the bottom, a door presented itself, to the lock of which she applied one of the keys, and then another, until she found one that opened it, and, although the key was exceedingly rusty, the lock turned with great ease.

The room, into which they now entered was one of the most dismal they had yet seen. It was paved with stone, was long and narrow, with a gothic window in a recess on the right side. The dim light which it admitted was almost obscured by the ivy on the outside; and the dark and overgrown boughs of a yew tree hanging close to it, gave a most melancholy appearance to the whole. Indeed Laura, for the first time, felt a shuddering at the idea of she knew not what; and Mary begged her to leave the room, and proceed no further; for a dark passage, or cloister, without a door, presented itself at the end of the room, and was neither floored or paved, but seemed to lead to some subterraneous abode.

Laura endeavoured to summon all her courage, and, regardless of her companion's entreaties, was venturing to explore the cloister, when a rustling noise made her start, and retreat from the low arch which led to its entrance.

Mary screamed with affright, and stood with her hands held before her eyes, lest they should encounter some sight too terrific for her to support. Laura likewise trembled; the boughs of the yew tree waved their dark branches against the window, and the whole appearance of the place augmented her fears. She took her companion's arm, and was hastily preparing to return, when a large trunk, or coffer, which stood in one corner of the room, attracted her notice, and she instantly accounted for the rustling, by supposing that a rat or mouse might be withinside of it; and, as this idea dispelled her fears, and renewed her courage, she advanced to the place where it stood, determined to lift up the lid, and see what it contained.[13] She did so; but

---

[13] A coffer is a strongbox or a large wooden crate used for storage.

how was she struck with horror and astonishment, when the skeleton of a human body presented itself to her affrighted view! She gave an involuntary scream, and dropping the lid from her trembling hand, the sound, echoing through the hallow roof, vibrated with terror upon her palpitating heart; and she had just sufficient power to say to Mary, in a tremulous voice, "Let us be gone."

Mary, who had not seen what the trunk contained, but remained some paces behind, with her hands covering her eyes, on perceiving that Laura had discovered something frightful, was still more alarmed, and hastily advanced to make an escape from a room, which, from the first moment she beheld it, had filled her with apprehensions.

Laura had just strength enough to lock the door, and then proceeded back again to their own apartment, which, in comparison with those they had been viewing, appeared light and pleasant.

Mary congratulated herself on her return, and told Laura she hoped she had now enough of exploring the Abbey, which presented nothing but dismal places and frightful objects; and she had no doubt was haunted by some of the people who had, she was sure, been murdered there; nor had she any doubts but their ghosts would appear at night, and inform them who were their murderers.

Laura begged she would not give way to such idle fancies. "That I have been frightened," says she, "I confess; and I also confess, that I am ashamed of myself for being so. A little reason and recollection will conquer my fears, and enable me, at some future day, to put my design in execution, and survey every part of the Abbey. What was there to fear in seeing the bones of a fellow creature, whose peaceful ashes were as quietly deposited there as in the mouldering earth? As to ghosts, she believed in no such thing; it was not the dead from whom she had any apprehensions, and she would never believe that the righteous Judge of all the earth, and on whom alone she placed her confidence, would suffer her to be visited and terrified for the sins of former ages. If any necessary discoveries were to be made thro' her means, she might, and ought to be thankful for being considered as an instrument worthy to bring good out of evil. That we should be alarmed at the sight of our fellow-creatures, when they had no longer any power to hurt us, was a sad proof of the weakness and depravity of our nature, and she owned she felt the force of that depravity in having been so much frightened at what she had seen; and although she could not boast of any superior courage, yet it shewed her the necessity of making the utmost of that reason which had been so liberally diffused in our compositions for the best and wisest purposes." Thus she reasoned, and having no one to oppose her arguments (for Mary sat in silent admiration of her judgement and eloquence), she had worked herself up to a kind of enthusiastic courage, and said she would again venture to complete her design, and would not even ask Mary to accompany her, if she had any fears; for her own part she felt equal to the attempt, and was rising in order to put her design in execution, when Mary besought her to desist: "Pray," says she, "defer it till Dame Giles comes at dinner time, and perhaps she will go with you; for, as myself, I cannot accompany you, and I should be as much afraid to stay here alone."

Laura allowed herself to be persuaded, and had less difficulty in getting Mary to take a walk with her on the outside of the Abbey before the sun went down, for she had no sort of objection to turning her back upon so dismal an abode, and would have been heartily glad never to have set her foot in the inside any more. They accordingly proceeded down the staircase, and out of the door through which they had entered the preceding night.

Laura had now an opportunity of observing, that the Abbey was situated in a deep valley, surrounded by hills of an enormous and stupendous height, whose craggy tops seemed to bend over the space that contained a few scattered cottages, which, with a small old church and the Abbey, formed the whole of the village. She proceeded to a rising ground to the right of the building, from whence she had a more perfect view of the Abbey, the length of which appeared to be some hundred feet, though it seemed much longer than it really was from the lowness of the structure. The church was a building of the same date; duty was sometimes performed in it by a neighbouring clergyman, but it appeared, as well as the Abbey, in a very decayed state. A low arch, or cloister, seemed to run from the right wing of the Abbey, and joined the church yard.

Upon examining the situation of the windows, and particularly the yew-tree near one of them, Laura was convinced that this arch was the same that enclosed the passage, or cloister, which led from the dismal room wherein she had seen the skeleton; and she again reprobated her fears when she considered that, as the cloister communicated with the church-yard, it was easy to suppose a skeleton might well be conveyed to a place so near it, for want of room, or for some other reasons; and vexed that this idea had not occurred to her sooner, she again condemned her fearfulness, and determined to make a second attempt as soon as another day presented itself.

The hour now approaching when the day began to get dreary, and observing Dame Giles coming to prepare their dinner, she proposed to Mary to return to the Abbey, who followed her companion, although with reluctance; for she had much rather have encountered the inclemency of the weather, or any other inconvenience, than again venture into the gloomy Abbey; the whole of and, although she made several attempts to visit the room, which contained the skeleton, she never found her courage quite equal to the enterprise; and, though she reasoned upon the absurdity of her fears, and determined to go there, yet her steps generally led to the room where she had found the letter-case, and where the beautiful picture always attracted her admiration, and engaged her stay.

Meantime Lord Oakendale grew impatient that he heard nothing from her. The footman had several times been dispatched to the village in order to enquire how she bore her solitude, and if she made no complaints; for Lord Oakendale was in hopes that, by placing her in this dreary Abbey, with no companion but Mary, (whose education and manner of life had not been such as could render her mind congenial with Laura's) as she could have no resources from books, or any other amusement, her spirits would become so depressed, and her mind so enervated,[16] that she would gladly fly to him for succour and friendship, rather than be condemned to a hateful solitude, like that of Oakendale Abbey.

Laura's character he had quite mistaken, or rather he had no idea of so noble a mind inhabiting a form which he considered only as a voluptuary. Finding, therefore that the footman always returned with accounts of her being contented, and making no complaints, he

---

[16] To weaken or destroy strength or vitality.

determined, as soon as the spring should be a little advanced, to make her a visit at the Abbey; and not without the diabolical idea, that, if he could not prevail upon her to be favourable to his wishes, the Abbey was a place well calculated for the very worst designs.

These intentions, however, were confined to his own breast, as the safest receptacle for them. Not the most distant hint was given of his intention, least Laura, upon hearing it, might meditate an escape, although that was a circumstance next to impossible to be effected, from the situation of the place.

Meantime as the days grew longer, she frequently walked with Mary to the distance of a mile or two; the views were picturesque, and romantic; and when she climbed to the top of the hills she had a prospect of a beautiful lake, which sometimes afforded her a distant hope of escape, as she had heard that these lakes were visited in the summer by the admirers of picturesque landscape. The Abbey lost much of its horrors by being inhabited by so fair a form, and the peasants of the village would now venture as far as the gate, and even peep in at the windows, divested of their former fears.[17] When the weather was rainy, Laura made a long gallery in the Abbey her walk, and Mary grew so fearless that she would remain in the chamber by herself, although

---

[17] Laura's presence transforms the horrific Abbey and dispels its terror. Its mythic legend weakens and the Abbey slowly becomes approachable by those who feared it before Laura's arrival.

led to no discovery, for she could see but one shadow; and having, by degrees, and by reasoning upon the impossibility, conquered every idea of fear it had first occasioned, she again resumed her intention of looking at the room which contained the skeleton.

One day, that had been uncommonly rainy, which had prevented her taking her favourite walk upon the hill, and her mind was unsettled, from having no employment to fill up the time, or to chase away the melancholy which her situation inspired, after much consideration, she determined to bend her steps down the stone stair-case. For this purpose she summoned all her resolution, and having, with fervent devotion, recommended herself to that Power, who always protects the innocent, and where mercy is infinite, she preceded to the room, the lock of which turned easily as before; she surveyed it with composed attention. The trunk stood exactly in the same place; she lifted up the lid, and the same ghastly skeleton presented itself to her view. She contemplated it with a mixture of horror and pity. "Ah!" says she, "would I could know what body enveloped these bones; perhaps thou art entitled to my tenderest regards." The idea that it might be the remains of the murdered, loved, Eugene, occurred to her sad memory, and the tears fell from her eyes in large drops upon the object which excited them.

From this melancholy spectacle she turned to the dark cloister which, as she supposed, led to the church yard. The gloomy appearance of the entrance for a moment intimidated her, and she was almost inclined to go back, when a ray of courage enlivening her spirits, she grew resolute and determined to proceed. She stooped her head as she entered the arch, and found it quite dark; but as she advanced it grew lighter, and she perceived that she descended, and the roof then admitted of her standing upright. She likewise found that the light proceeded from some opening at the end, which she conjectured was the open air, and that the end of the cloister would bring her to the church-yard; she therefore boldly advanced, when, upon a nearer approach, she perceived that the light glimmered through some loose boards in the form of a partition, without a door, or any apparent opening. She looked through the cracks, and perceived it was a room, and that the light proceeded from a casement at the end of it. She pushed hard against it, in order to get in; but it seemed beyond her strength. She felt disappointed, and was turning back the way she had come, when an impulse of curiosity impelled her once more to look through the cracks of the boards, in order to take amore accurate survey of a place which seemed fenced off for some particular purpose. She then fancied she saw something like white linen hang up on the opposite side; but she could not distinguish it perfectly, as the confined place through which she looked unfrequented parts of the Abbey to whisper and make noises to occasion terror. The skeleton, the shadow, and the eye-ball, might be managed by his Lordship's contrivance; consequently they lost their terror, and she looked upon all that was past as an artful delusion, pre-concerted to further and complete his purpose; she therefore, as heretofore, condemned herself for being so easily imposed upon, and determined henceforward to disregard all appearances, and if possible to think of making her escape.

With respect to Mary she did not think her sufficiently in her interest to trust her with any scheme she might project; neither did she possess courage, or strength of mind, to be of service to her in any dangerous enterprise; she therefore thought it most prudent to rely upon her own management, and entirely trust to her own contrivance for the furthering of any plan, by which she might hope to escape from a situation so perilous.[23]

She had, by these suggestions, worked up her mind to a degree of boldness, bordering upon desperation; and, in a rhapsody of distressed courage, she exclaimed, "Would some airy spirit did indeed inhabit this Abbey, who would protect innocence, and shield me from the snares villainy and terror!"

As she finished the last words, she was startled by a noise like the shutting of a door, and a distant footstep;

---

[23] Laura's insight to self preservation in not simply passive intuition—it is pre-meditated thought, foresight, and intelligent deductive reasoning.

but, as she had made up her mind to disregarding the noises, and indeed fear of that nature seemed to be entirely banished from her breast, she only turned about with a contemptuous expression of countenance, and fell into a meditation on her escape. As she had never been prohibited walking round the Abbey, up the hills and in the vicinity of the village, she formed the resolution of extending her walk so as to get quite away, taking the first path that offered, after she had got from the village.

The idea charmed her, and but one difficulty arose to prevent her design; and that was, the walking out by herself, as Mary had always been her companion in the walks she had hitherto taken, and indeed would be afraid to be left alone in the Abbey.

The idea of leaving one, whose fears she knew would nearly overpower her senses, was not only matter of difficulty, but of regret; and she truly felt for the distress Mary would experience when night approached, and she found herself alone, deserted by her companion.

The tender and affectionate heart of Laura could not endure the idea of acting so cruel a part to one, who in no instance had ever shewn her the least unkindness. To be sure her virtue where of that negative kind, that she could for: no reliance upon her friendship, but then, on the other hand, she had been in some degree, the chosen companion of her solitude, and to leave her prey to sufferings her mind was not able to support, was a cruelty of which Laura was incapable, and could not put the apartments they occupied before Mary should have quitted them; for, although her fears were pretty well subsided, yet the idea of being alone all night in the Abbey was not altogether so comfortable; and she thought, if Mary was gone, she would follow her to the cottage of Aaron Giles. She was not deceived as to the door at the other end of the room; it was fastened on the side next to her, and she undrew (as she thought) a rusty bolt, and was advancing into another apartment, when a sight more horrible than imagination can form, presented itself to her. The dead body of a woman hung against the wall opposite to the door she had entered, with a coarse cloth pinned over all but the face; the ghastly and putrefied appearance of which bespoke her to have been some time dead.[25]

Laura gave a fearful shriek, when a tall figure, dressed only in a checked shirt, staggered towards her. The face was almost black; the eyes seemed starting from the

---

[25] The strange white linen object explained! (See page 62). In a powerful Gothic trope, Carver forces our attention on real, grotesque horror—The mysterious object is explained, but it is more horrific than we may have imagined. Like the Gothic writers before her, Carver explains the image, but accentuates the depraved and the grotesque where many other writers would relieve the fear by explaining the linen cloth as being merely a curtain or a drape rather than a rotting female corpse hung upon the wall like a hideous decoration. Additionally, like Blue Beard's final wife, Laura's curiosity has driven her to a chamber of horrors and dead women. For more information on Feminist theory and classic fairy tales, see Marina Warner's engrossing study *From the Beast to the Blonde: On Fairy Tales and Their Tellers.*

head; the mouth was widely extended, and made a kind of hallow guttural sound in attempting to articulate.

Laura stood motionless; the figure passed her, and went through the door-way by which she had entered, and the sound of the footsteps dwelt upon her ear till they seemed lost by distance. She trembled exceedingly; she was afraid to follow and she was equally afraid to stay. After some moments of dreadful suspence, she turned her eyes to the shocking figure of the dead body; nature shrunk from the sight, and recoiled at the idea; she moved slowly to the door, thinking, if she could once more regain the wood, she should be more safe than where she was. Alas! how were her fears increased, and her situation rendered still more dreadful, when she found (upon attempting to open the door) a spring lock on the other side had been mistaken for a bolt; that it was now close shut and she had no possible means of getting it open. The horrid creature that had passed her had gone through with so much violence that the door clapped after him, whilst she was contemplating the other dreadful figure with which she was now shut up; nothing could be conceived more full of terror! The room was damp, and a small grated window only served to shew her the ghastly appearance of the body, rendered still more terrific by the faint light which reflected on the face, and served to shew Laura that night was approaching. Her fears increased; she crept about the room as far as possible from the melancholy object, and kept her eyes turned to the door of this dismal place, from whence she had not the most distant hope of making her escape.

With a mind tortured by the most cruel apprehensions, she could think of no expedient whereby to relieve her distress. She made several attempts to open the door, but all were ineffectual. The little strength she had was become still less by trembling, and a faint sickness occasioned by terror. She shut her eyes to avoid the painful object before her. She fancied she heard groans. The idea of perishing for want was the least of her fears. About midnight she heard footsteps gently approaching the door; a glimmering light shone under it, and displayed more fully the horror of her situation, all her courage was summoned to her aid, and all her courage could scarce support her in this extremity of danger. She had turned her back upon the dead body, as an object too shocking to look at; and she now crept up in a corner of the room, on the same side with the door, where she stood close, still hoping to escape from she knew not what; but the love of life is so strongly implanted in our nature, that when the alarm of death comes, under whatsoever circumstances, we make the last attempts to preserve it, however feeble they may be.

Thus she stood trembling, awaiting a fate which she every moment expected would be decided, when the door gently opened, and two men entered; the one carried a lantern, and the other a large board; and, as with astonished looks, they advanced towards her; her heart died within her, she sunk down, and saw and heard no more!

On recovering she found herself laid on a coarse bed, with an old woman standing by her, whose looks testified satisfaction when she opened her eyes. As soon as she could speak, she inquired "if she was still in Oakendale Abbey?"

"No," said the woman; "you are in my cottage, and I have been fearfully frightened lest you were dead."

"Thank God," said Laura, "I am once more with a human being; and pray tell me by what, or whose means I came here?"

"Lawkaday!" said the woman; "I knows no more than you do: Christian charity made me take you in, when two men brought you here to be recovered. They assured me you was not dead, and would be better in a short time; I was loth to trust them, and now I'm afraid I shall get into trouble; for I thinks you be the same Lady that has lived so long with the spirits in the Abbey."

"Whatever I am," said Laura, "I entreat you to tell me how far I am from that hateful Abbey, and if there is a road leads to it from the little wood?"

"Aye, sure there is," said the woman, "and it is hard by. Laws! I don't wonder you have been almost frightened to death, if you have been in that shocking place; why, nobody before ever ventured to stay there."

"Nine miles," said John; "and I would no go there at this time o'night for all you could give me."

"Nor I neither," thought Laura to herself, surprised that she had walked so far.

"No," said the wife, "that is a fearful place by all account; such frightful sights ha been seen there, as makes a body shake but to think on; and bloody murders ha been committed there formerly no doubt!"

If Laura was satisfied and pleased with her host and hostess, they were not less so with her gentle manners and obliging behaviour; and entertained no suspicion to the disadvantage of their guest, whom they pressed to partake of the best they had to produce; and she joyfully shared the coarse, but clean, bed of Mary Ann.

The next morning, not knowing where to bend her course, and thinking she should be more secure from Lord Oakendale's search, should he be disposed to make any after her, under some safe protection, she listened to the advice of the cottagers, and begged they would conduct her to the Grove, where resided the good lady of whom they had spoken so highly, and whose name was Greville. The Grove was situated about a mile from the cottage, and the towers of that antient structure peeped from between the lofty elms and oaks that encompassed its structure, and gave it its name.

As they approached the mansion, Laura ruminated on the mode of introducing herself to the lady of the house, and could devise no better than by declaring the truth, and entreating her protection, which from the cottager's reports she was encouraged to hope would not be denied her.

When they arrived at the house they were received by the house-keeper, a comely looking woman, about fifty years of age, dressed in a plain old fashion style, with a bunch of keys by her side. When Laura requested to be introduced to Mrs. Greville, the house-keeper asked "who she was to name."

Laura blushed, and a tear started into her eyes upon the recollection that she knew no name to which she had any just claim; and, with a sigh returned, "I have been taught to believe that the name of Unfortunate will introduce me to your lady, and secure me a favourable reception."

The house-keeper, glancing an eye of pity on her, led the way, and introduced her to Mrs Greville, a venerable old lady, who, taking off her spectacles, politely said, "I have not the honor of knowing you, young lady; but that, I dare say, is owning to the defect of my sight and memory."

"Alas! no," replied Laura; but here her forlorn situation recurring to her mind too forcibly to be suppressed, she again burst into tears. Perhaps this was the best introduction she could have chosen as a passport to the tender heart of Mrs. Greville. She looked at Laura with the eyes of pity, and taking her by the hand, said, in the kindest accents, "Sit down, young lady, and compose yourself; you seem fatigued, and shall take some refreshment before you gratify a curiosity, which is, I own, strongly excited, and be assured, prejudiced in your favour."

Saying this, she dismissed the house-keeper for some chocolate; and, in the mean time, Laura so far recovered herself as to say, "Dear Madam, you see before you a forlorn creature thrown upon the world, without country, friends, or fortune, to protect me; not even a relation from whom I can claim either name or affinity!"

"Then," said Mrs. Greville, "surely you are the more entitled to the protection of strangers."

Laura thanked her by the most grateful acknowledgements; and, having drank her chocolate, began the following history of herself:

"My infant remembrance," said she, "furnishes me with ideas of a country different from this. A gentleman, caressing me, in scarlet clothes, with a sash and gorget,[27] and other glittering appendages, dazzled my young sight, and made an impression on my memory like a distant dream. I can recollect a beautiful woman snatching me to her arms when the gentleman was gone; and, as she kissed me, the tears fell from her eyes in drops upon my frock. I remember too that I was called Laura. The next circumstance that dwelt upon my recollection, was that of sitting upon the lap of a black woman, who told me I

---

[27] A gorget is an ornamental collar.

should see my papa and mama no more; that I must be very good, and she would love me. She taught me my prayers, and the meaning of words; but she omitted to tell me my name. She treated me with great tenderness, and I conceived an affection for her. Soon after she put me on board a ship with several people of my own colour; and, after hugging and embracing me with great affection, she left me. I cried after her as the only being of whom I had any knowledge, and I could not easily be reconciled to any other. The motion of the vessel first made me sick, and then lulled me to sleep. When I awoke I cried again; but was soothed by some women on board, and told that I was going to see my relations. I soon grew accustomed to the ship, and to the people about me, although I was too young to understand any of their conversation, or know whither we were going. As far as my early age, and distance of time, would allow me to judge, we were some months at sea; when one morning I was frightened by a confused noise, which was followed by a continued firing of cannon. The whole ship's crew seemed in alarm, and I was huddled with the rest of the women, into a dark part of the vessel, which I had never been seen before. Every one seemed terrified, and felt the contagion of fear, though I knew not what we had to dread. In a short time a number of men, who spoke in a different language to that I had been used to, and were almost without clothes, rushed into the place where we were confined and began to drag the women about, in whose screams and cries I joined: All appeared in confusion, when two or three better dressed men came, and, speaking in a commanding tone, there seemed to be more regulation observed; but they did not trouble themselves with me, expect to shut me in with the rest.

"Previous to this ceremony, and upon hearing a shout, in what I afterwards knew to be the French language, one of the women took a sealed packet from a trunk, which she said belonged to me, and with a string fastened it round my body, telling me (for I shall remember her words) that was the only testimony of my name and parentage; adding, that I must never let any body take it from me. Her intention was no doubt good, but she would no doubt have done better to have taught me my name, and so impressed it on my memory, that I might not now have been the destitute and forlorn creature I feel myself; but I was then too young to observe the omission.

"Soon after this we arrived, as I suppose, at our destined port, where we were dragged out of the vessel, and put into wagons; when, after a tedious journey of several days, during which I suffered cold and hunger to the extreme; we were at length brought to a large city, which I heard was Paris. If I was before wretched, though at that time I felt the sensation without knowing by what name to describe it, how much was my misery increased when we were all crammed into a French prison.

"On my first being taken out of the wagon, a tall frightful man, with a wide mouth, held me in his arms, and made a motion as if he would eat me! I was terrified, and cried; but no cries were regarded, and we were hurried into the prison, which contained some hundreds of wretches like ourselves. My clothes and linen were of a finer texture than those of my companions; I was therefore, regardless of my cries, stripped, and clad in a very coarse and filthy garb. I held the paper, which was tied round me, fast with my little hands; but I was brutally forced to relinquish my hold, and it was wantonly torn from me. After this I remembered nothing for many days; I turned my head this way, and that way, to avoid the stench of the prison; but could in no direction find a wholesome air. When I recovered, from what I suppose was a fever and delirium, I found myself stretched upon a wretched bed with several others, and some of the dead bodies were removing to their last abode. I understood none of the language, and my first wish was for fresh air. As I was lying in this miserable condition, a gentleman entered the room, whose countenance and appearance was different from what I had seen before. He felt the pulse of some of them, and spoke the language I understood. I wished to attract his notice, and my eyes followed his countenance whithersoever it turned. At last he approached the bed on which I was laid, and, coming to the side of it, examined my features with attention.

"I longed to speak to him; but I had scarce strength, and still less courage to make such an effort; but when he took by burning emaciated hand in his I ventured to clasp his fingers whilst the tears streamed from my eyes.

"He tenderly returned the pressure, saying, "Poor child, to whom dost thou belong? and what is thy name?"

"I faintly answered, Laura; and I am very sick. He gave me something which he poured out of a bottle, and which seemed of a reviving quality; and when the person, who attended the room three or four times a day, and locked us up, came in, he conferred with him several minutes in the French language, frequently pointing to me as he spoke.

"The next morning an old woman, whom I had before seen busy about the bodies of those that died in the room, came and took me from the bed, washed me, and put upon me some coarse but clean linen, led to me out into the air, and gave me some better refreshment than I had lately tasted. I was then put into a coach in which sat the gentleman I had seen the day before. He spoke to me in the kindest accents, and I endeavoured to shew my gratitude by a thousand childish endeavours.

"When the coach stopped, I was led by my benefactor into a handsome room, where sat a lady of a most benign countenance: "this my dear," said the gentleman, leading me to her, "is the poor child of whom I spoke yesterday, and whom you have so kindly consented to receive; she has been very ill and is weak at present; but I am sure she has a grateful heart."

"I paid my respects to the lady in the best manner I was able; and she said, "Poor thing, she shall be taken care of; and I think she looks like a gentleman's child." I felt my heart glow with pleasure at this observation; and I will confess, that it gave me more delight than all the caresses they bestowed.

"In a few days I was still better habited; and I told my benefactors, whose names were du Frene, all that I knew and could remember of my history. They had no children, and they conceived a parental regard for me, which I returned by the most the filial affection. They were French; but he was of the English extraction, and both were Protestants. He had resided many years in Paris, where he practiced surgery, and had been in high repute in that profession, and which he now followed from motives of humanity rather than from lucrative ones, as he was in very good of circumstances.

"My dear Madame du Frene was the only mother I had ever known. She grew every day more fond of me. She had me taught every necessary accomplishment, as well as every useful employment; and the principles of religion and virtue, which he practiced in their fullest extent, she instilled—into my mind is the brightest ornaments I could possess.—Indeed, they appeared with such lustre, from her bright example, that I wanted no incitements to be at least and humble imitator of her many virtues. Were I to dwell upon all her excellencies, my story would not soon come to conclusion. Nor had the Mons. du Frene less merit; I know not which of them shewed me most fondness; and when I grew up, their tender care of me, as a child, was changed into unremitting anxiety and solicitude. When I was addressed by the appellation of Mademoiselle du Frene, their eyes sparkled with pleasure; and this was often the case, for I knew no other name; and after all the inquiries M. du Frene will could make, concerning the parcel which was fastened to my breast on my entrance into the prison, no discovery could possibly be made regarding to it; for which reason it was natural to suppose that it contained something valuable—besides the identity of my birth and name, which alone we should have no difficulty in recovering.—Whenever I expressed uneasiness at the circumstances of not knowing whom I owed my being, with what enraptured fondness would these dear parents call me their adopted child, and assure me that I should never feel the want of such endearing ties! I hope I returned their affection by the most filial love and duty; but youth is giddy, and we never know the value of a blessing till it is no longer in our power to set a just estimate upon it. Ten years endeared me to this kind protection, upon which I look back with delight. I learned to speak the language fluently, though English was as much spoken in M. du Frene's family as French. No expence was spared on my education, dress, or amusement, and I moved in a circle far above the sphere of life in which M. du Frene was placed; but it was their pride to have me introduced, and see me caressed by people of rank; and M. du Frene was well-received by these persons on account of his extraordinary merit.

"It was in the midst of these happy days, when much to do friend received letters from his brother in England, who was in the same profession, apprising him a of the arrival of a young gentleman, of the name Rayneer, who was sent to be under his care, in order to be made a proficient in the language, and to complete his education.

"I was in the habit of hearing fine things from the beaux who fluttered around me in public places, and sometimes distinguished a man of sense and good breeding from the empty coxcomb and the licentious rake; but none had made an impression beyond the moment in which they addressed me, and my heart had never as yet palpitated in favour of one man more than another; but the time was now approaching when I could no longer make this boast. Eugene Rayneer arrived; his figure, his voice, his manner, all were captivating in the extreme. He did not live under the same roof with me; but he had lodgings near us, and there were but few hours out of the twenty-four in which we were not together. Ah! how dangerous it is to throw into each other's company two young people nearly of an age, and between whose dispositions a similarity of sentiments cannot fail to form attachment!—what pleasant hours did we pass together! But I will not, dear Madame, tire you with a repetition of our love, the remembrance of which is painful because it is past. Suffice it to say, that we exchanged mutual vows without considering the improbability there was of our ever been united. He seemed to know but little of his family, and still less of his fortune: but nature had been abundantly lavish of her favours, and his own endeavours had not been wanting to render him a most accomplished young man. His temper was generous and good, but rather inclined to be impetuous. My dear M. du Frene used frequently to lament that he had not sufficient authority over him to keep him from errors occasioned by this disposition.

"One day that we were at dinner M. du Frene was suddenly, and with an air of mystery, called out. He instantly obeyed the summons, and did not return for some time. I knew not what passed in the mind of Madame; but my own heart foreboded a thousand fearful images during an hour's absence of M. du Frene. At his return we both expressed curiosity at the face of anxiety with which he appeared: and, after a few moments of silence, he said, "that Foolish boy Eugene, has engaged in a disagreeable adventure, and has got an ugly wound in the recontre."

"At the mention of a wound I felt my blood rush into my face, and a violent beating of my heart succeeded. He went on by saying, "He hoped there was no danger in the wound; but he understood it was the consequence of a challenge given by Eugene to a person of consequence, who was likewise wounded, and whose friends he feared would not easily be appeased." What terror did these words convey to my already oppressed mind! Several days passed in this cruel uncertainty. Madame du Frene frequently visited Eugene; but she always returned with a melancholy countenance, and I had scarce ever courage to ask her any questions.

"One day she returned with cheerful looks, and mine caught the pleasing sympathy. She put out her hand to me, and said, "My dear Laura, I can now congratulate you on the complete recovery of Eugene. At the same time I will inform you, that you have been the cause of a wound which had nearly been fatal.

"How, my dear Madame," I replied, "can I have been the cause of such an accident? and, if I have, how ought I to rejoice that the danger is over?"

"Sit down, my love," said Madame; "be composed, and I will tell you the whole. Eugene was playing at billiards with the young Marquis of—, only son of the Duke de St.—. They have played several games, and the Marquis, having been successful, was very desirous that Eugene should win some of the games back again; but Eugene wanted to be with you, he grew impatient, and uttering some hasty words, the Marquis replied, "Oh! you want to be with that little Bourjeoise, the surgeon's daughter; ah! she is a tempting little creature; but she may wait till our games are more evenly decided."

"Eugene heard no more. He instantly gave the challenge, and they as instantly ran each other through the body. Both fell at the same moment, and would have both died from loss of blood, had not one of the waiters fortunately discovered them. It would be impossible to say which of their wounds was most dangerous. The symptoms of the Marquis were most favourable, because his mind was not so agitated as Eugene; nevertheless they were both extremely dangerous, and the Duke of — would have shewn no favour to his son's antagonist had he lost him. Thank God they are now in a fairway of recovery, and both have exchanged forgiveness; and till this favourable event, M. du Frene and myself have preserved a strange and unpleasant silence towards you; but, unless we could give you more favourable accounts, we were determined to keep you in ignorance. But now, that everything is in so prosperous a train, we would have you partake in the general joy."

"I thanked my dear Madame, by the most grateful acknowledgements, for all her kindness; and my heart overflowed with praise and thanksgiving for my Eugene's recovery. I longed to see him, but I had not courage to make the request. Madame du Frene anticipated my wishes, and said, "There can, I think, be no impropriety in your going with me to see Eugene; I know the sight of you will complete his cure."

"I wanted no intreaty to pay a visit in which my heart was so much interested; and I had the pleasure of finding Eugene perfectly well, except weakness. To me he never looked or spoke in a more captivating manner. In a few days he walked out; our interviews were more frequent than ever, and I foolishly thought that all misfortune was comprehended in the illness of Eugene; and now, that he was well and again restored to me, I had nothing but happiness before me. Alas! how little do we know how fortune varies her favour, and dispenses a chequered scene to most mortals.—I could not divest myself of extreme partiality for Eugene, and found a pleasure in his company, which I had never experienced from the frivolity of a Frenchman; and when the most sensible remarks, and the tenderest attentions, were received from a man whose external appearance bespoke the nobler qualities of his mind, my heart gave the truest testimony to his merits; nor did I affect to disown them to my dear Madame du Frene; to her I had confided all my grief, and all my joy. She would allow me to expatiate on the merits of my beloved Eugene with all the glow of affection which warmed my breasts; she loves me too tenderly to check the fond effusions which afforded me so much delight; and when I fancied that I was possessed of his affections, nothing I thought, could interrupt my happiness, or reverse my fortune:—She would only insinuate in the gentlest accents, and with the most is persuasive arguments, that I must not expect complete happiness; that all our lives were liable to the caprice of fortune, and whose changes human nature was born to encounter, and must submit.—Perfect bliss was the lot of none, nor was even a large portion of happiness possessed by many; she would therefore wish to prepare my mind, and make it equal to meet the dispensations of all human events, that so I might secure that peace, which the world can neither give nor take away.

"Thus was I, by her dear precepts, in some decree fitted for those many difficulties and dangers I have already encountered; and to her, next to God Almighty, I am indebted did for this fortitude which has hitherto sustained to me." But to return to my story.

"One morning Eugene shewed me a letter he had received, which recalled him to England. He said it came from a gentleman who was his guardian, and whom he was bound to obey. There were some sentences in the letter, which were couched in such terms as lead us both to think, that when the writer talked of forming improper connexions, by remaining too long in one place, he alluded to our intimacy.

"Eugene at first declared he would not obey the mandate, and that he had long enough submitted to the controul and caprice of those whom he really believed had no right to direct, or take any part in his conduct. As to myself, I was totally incapable of giving advice; but there was no occasion; M. du Frene decided for us. He also had received a letter on the same subject, and Eugene's fate was determined. If ever there was a moment in which my love for M. du Frene was abated, it was when he peremptorily told him he must not delay his departure. I felt as if I had received a blow, which deprived me of all my faculties; nor could all the assurances of Eugene's faith and everlasting love reconcile me to the idea of losing him. I considered his departure as the deprivation of all my happiness; nor could all that the admonitions of Madame calm my feelings. Indeed those dear parents lamented his lost almost as much as myself; and when the day arrived on which he was too taking his leave, I scarce knew which of us were most concerned.

"M. du Frene pressed him to his heart, and conjured him never to forget friends to whom he was so dear; and Madame said a thousand kind and affectionate things to him. As to myself, I stood like a picture of despair; and when Eugene pressed me to his bosom, I felt as if my whole existence was at an end, and I could not articulate a sentence. Ah! too just was my presentment that we should never meet again. He promised to write, and (if possible) to return; but never, from that sad hour, did we hear or see any more of him; and from that time happiness seemed to have fled with my lost Eugene.

"M. du Frene was a politician. What grief did that circumstance occasion to Madame! We use all our persuasions to keep them at home, and take no part in the broils which began to be very general; but it was to no purpose that we urged him to be neuter; he was too much attached to his king to bear quietly the disaffection which prevailed, and every where began to spread itself. All our entreaties were used in vain; a whole year passed in this unpleasant state, and no intelligence of Eugene arrived to soothe the tedious hours, rendered still more irksome by M. du Frene's frequent quarrels and uneasiness, by the melancholy which always pervaded his countenance, and the continued read we were under of some new calamity happening to the state.

"In this distressed condition we continued till the fatal tenth of August, 1792; that era of ever—lasting disgrace to the French nation, when Paris was deluged in human gore.[28] On that sad day M. du Frene had gone from home early in the morning, and I had been vainly endeavouring to persuade Madame du Frene that her fears were needless, when a loud knocking at the door, and a tumult, made me venture to look through the window; when ah! how does my soul sicken at the remembrance! I saw my ever dear, my more than parent's head, stuck upon a pike, reeking and clotted with blood! I uttered a scream, and hid my eyes with my hands; when Madam du Frene coming to my assistance, discovered the dreadful object which had occasioned my

---

[28] The Reign of Terror begins in France. The French Revolution (1793-1794) was marked by brutal repression and bloody internal conflict. Current historians believe that between 18,500 and 40,000 people were executed.

terror! She gave a piercing scream, which, methinks, now vibrates on my ear, and dropped senseless on the floor.

"Greatly as I was affected, I exerted myself to assist and recall her to live, which it was some time before she shewed any signs of. When she and some degree, recovered, she observed a profound silence upon the subject of the horrible sight we had both of us but to plainly seen. Her size, indeed, were deep and bitter; but it seemed as if she could not bear to name the shocking circumstance which occasioned them, and to which she must have been witness. We had scarce time to recollect ourselves, and my dear Madame du Frene shewed but little signs of animation, when some of our friends assembled at our house, and earnestly entreated we would lose no time in making our escape, if we wished to avoid the cruel fate which some of those dearest to us had experienced. We neither of us seemed sufficiently interested to prolong our wretchedness or attend to their remonstrance's, and we appeared rather to wish for death then to avoid it; but our friends used such pressing solicitations, and begged so earnestly, that we would leave Paris with them, that we began (though reluctantly) to put up our valuables, and to prepare for our departure. Little as I cared for life, or had an prospect to invite its continuance, yet the name of England sounded with a sweet sensation. A thousand tender ideas were associated with that country; and the fond remembrance of Eugene played around my heart amidst

the sorrows that encompassed me. I joined my
endeavours to rouse Madame du Frene from her lethargy
of woe, and to fly whilst it was yet in our power; and
having succeeded, we left Paris that night, and travelled
with as much expedition as the French carriages could
make, till we got to Boulogne, where we found this town
crowded with emigrants, waiting to cross the water.

"When the wind was fair, and the vessels were ready,
we were hurried down to the quay in such numbers, and
put on board in so much confusion, that I was
unfortunately separated from my dear Madame du Frene,
and put on board of a merchantman.

"As soon as I found myself separated from her, I
entreated, and offered largely to the captain if he would
set me onshore again; but he was deaf to all my cries, and
said he would not lose a moment. My misery was not to
be described! I found myself encompassed by strangers;
and what was worse, I understood we were to be set
shore on the Welch Coast.

"As to the fate of Madame du Frene, from that hour
to this, I have remained in total ignorance about it; and it
has been an everlasting cause of sorrow to me!

"We landed in Milford Haven, at a place which
appeared almost uninhabited; and consisted only of an
inn and near few houses. It might be considered as a
bathing place, but of little resort. I fixed my residence in
a small lodging near the sea, to which my eyes were

incessantly turned, in the hope of seeing some vessel which might bring Madame du Frene to the same spot.

"Most of the people who landed with me, disbursed to different parts of England; but as I could think of no place to prefer to this, I thought it best, for the present, to remain where I was. I was attended by a young woman of the village, named Mary Morgan; she was neat, and well behaved; and I passed most of my time in wandering with her on the beach. I wished to go to London, as the most likely place to hear of Madame du Frene; but I was afraid to go there alone, there not being in that vast metropolis one person with whom I could claim acquaintance.

"It happened one evening that, as I was walking upon the beach with Mary, I perceived myself observed by a good looking man, who appeared to be about 40 years of age, and who seemed to eye me with uncommon attention. There was something in his person and manners, which not only attracted my notice, but also my partiality. Our eyes met; and, as I was standing still on the beach, I was not displeased at being accosted by him with some general observations upon the place we were in, and the sea prospect, &c.

"The next day we met upon the same spot, when our conversation was again renewed. We talked on various subjects, and he told me his name was Thoranby; that he lived in London, and generally came every summer to some place of this kind for the benefit of sea-bathing, and to be retired.

"Upon his saying that he lived in London, I am prudently replied, "That of all places I wished to go there;" at the same time a telling him that part of my history which had separated me from my more than mother, and my ardent wish to find her again.

"He seemed pleased with the affectionate duty I expressed; and, after paying me some compliments on my extreme sensibility, he said, "He had a sister in London, who would, he was sure, be happy to receive me; and would unite her endeavor to mine in order to discover Madame du Frene." How did my heart overflow with gratitude at this unexpected invitation! Young and unacquainted as I was with the arts of man, I hastily accepted his offer: and, indeed, my joy and impatience to begin my journey was too conspicuous to be concealed. Accordingly it was agreed, that he should set out on the next day, in order to prepare his sister for my arrival; and that in three days after I should follow with Mary, who had agreed to accompany me to London.

"Nothing could exceed my eagerness and impatience for the arrival of the day on which I was to set out; and I scarcely gave myself time for proper rest, and none at all for reflection. The hope of meeting my dear Madame du Frene, together with that secret wish which still glowed in my bosom of hearing something of Eugene, was cherished with such fond imagination, that I had almost realized my wishes to a certainty; and when we entered London, my fancy had formed so many fair ideas, by which I was wholly engrossed, that I hardly at tended to the astonished exclamations of poor Mary, at the sight of the streets, number of people, carriages, &c. &c. which to me, who had lived so long in Paris, was nothing extraordinary; but when the carriage drove up to a very magnificent house in Portland Place, my heart felt an unusual oppression; and, for the first time, suggested to me the impropriety of following to London a person of whom I knew so little; however, reflections of this kind word now too late. The chaise stopped; the bell was rung, and two footmen, in splendid liveries, ushered me through the hall, up a stone staircase.

"My astonishment increased as I ascended the steps. Mr. Thornaby had told me he lived in a handsome house in London; but I had no idea it was so superb, still less that his sister lived in this elegant style. I fancied there must have been some mistake, and a variety of reflections rushed with rapidity upon my mind, and a thousand forebodings, of I knew not what, agitated me so much, that I fancied I did not hear distinctly whom the servant addressed.

"Mr. Thoranby (who then made his appearance) by the appellation of "my Lord;" but when he approached to receive me, with a malignant smile of exultation, my heart died within me, and I faintly exclaimed, "I am betrayed."

"It was in vain that his lordship endeavoured to soothe me, after having acknowledged that he had deceived me respecting his having a sister, as well as his name and rank. I at once saw my ruined the situation; and I exclaimed on the cruelty of his conduct, demanding immediate release. He pleaded the most ardent love, protesting that he could not live without me. Finding me deaf to his vows, and resolute in my determination, this wretched Lord Oakendale confessed to me that he was a married man!

"Yes, my dear Laura," says he, "you should pity rather than condemn a man who is united to a woman for whom he can conceive nothing but aversion, and who is in no respect calculated for domestic happiness, whilst his heart is enraptured by your virtues, and absolutely devoted to your service; nothing but this prior tye should prevent me from instantly offering you a vow at the altar. Let me, therefore, loveliest of women! Secure to you any other contract which shall be equally binding, and a most sacred promise to marry you the very moment it is in my power."

"I had scarce patience to hear him to the end— "Marry me! (I replied) is it possible that your vanity can suggest such an idea? Did you bring me here to dazzle me with your splendour, as a means to gain me to your purpose? When I first became acquainted with you, it was your age which secured my confidence; and now that I find you are such a depraved character—" I was proceeding; but I found I had touched a string the most discordant to his ear, that of his age.

"Peace, Madam," said he; "nor dare to insult me thus. Age, indeed I know, silly girl, that you are in my power; and if you provoke that power, I warn you to take the consequence." With these words he hastily could did the room, leaving me to reflect upon my distress situation, with the additional torment of self-accusation for having brought myself into his power.

"During two whole days I saw nothing of his lordship, though I learned from (who was still allowed to attend me) that he was in the house, and that all the servants had orders to obey me in everything, except assisting me to leave it. She likewise informed me, that lady Oakendale was no further from London than Hampstead. Various were my conjectures upon his conduct. Sometimes I thought he would relent, and give me my liberty; at others, that he was only meditating further mischief. I had no hope of making my escape; for the rooms I was allowed to occupy were not in the front of the house, and only looked into a close paved court, from whence I could not possibly get out, were I to attempt the windows. My mind was harassed by sleepless nights and continual fatigue.

"On the third morning Lord Oakendale entered the apartment; he shewed some degree of compassion at my pale and altered looks; and then said, "You have foolishly rejected all my offers; but surely that must proceed from hasty judgment, and because you have not well considered them. However as I cannot bring myself to part with you entirely, I have thought of a plan which will give you an opportunity of considering my offers more deliberately; and let me add, with less haughtiness. I mean to send you down to an old Abbey in Cumberland, with Mary to accompany you, or any other of my domestics whom you may prefer. It is true, you will be but ill accommodated; but for that you may thank your own obstinacy, and you will there have leisure to consider my proposals with the attention they deserve."

"The idea of an Abbey made me shudder; but when I considered I should be released from my present prison, and that he said not a word of going with me, I thought it most prudent to dissemble; I therefore told him, in a milder tone than I had spoken before, that I was ready to follow whithersoever my destiny should lead me; that I chose Mary for my companion, and that I would consider of what he had said with more moderation. A smile of approbation sat upon his countenance as I uttered the last sentence. He took me tenderly by the hand, and said, "Then I will instantly order the carriage to be got ready" and having assured him it should not wait for me, he quitted me to give the necessary orders.

"The moment he was gone, a gleam of satisfaction overspread my mind at the idea of leaving that detested house. At the same moment a transitory regret occurred at the thoughts of leaving London; that London to which

I had hastened with such rapidity and which probably contained all that was most dear to me; yet, to gain in some degree, my liberty, and to leave Lord Oakendale was my first object; and I resolved to make no more hasty determinations; nor even attempt to make my escape without a great deal of deliberation and circumspection. Mary consented to accompany me; but it was evidently with reluctance. The splendour of Lord Oakendale's establishment had attracted her admiration, and she wished to stay longer and see more; but she was a foolish uninformed creature, and on that score I excused her; and thinking she was a more trusty companion then any Lord Oakendale could furnish me with, I pressed her to accompany me; at the same time giving her some money for the services she had already done me, and in order to secure her future fidelity; we therefore stepped in to the carriage, which I found was loaded with provisions, that we might have no occasion to stop, except for change of horses. We were attended by two servants on horse-back, and such precautions taken, that it would have been in vain to have meditated an escape. How ardently did I wish to be attacked by robbers, as the only means I could foresee of gaining my liberty; but no such good fortune happening, we, after a fatiguing journey, arrived at Oakendale Abbey."—And here Laura continued to relate all the terrors she had experienced in that place, as well as the manner of escaping; not omitting to inform Mrs. Greville the circumstance of her finding the letter case she had given to Eugene.

When she had finished her story, Mrs. Greville said, "Indeed, my dear young lady, your story is replete with uncommon circumstances of distress; and I am as much interested by it, as I am surprised and entertained. If your appearance prejudiced me in your favour, your uncommon sufferings and merit entitle you my regard and protection, which you may be assured of possessing as long as you are disposed to continue under my roof.

"I have (continued the good lady) a nephew, who is married to a very amiable woman; his name is Sir George Orland, and they pass great part of the year with me; you will, I am sure, like each other, and if you pay them a visit in London, they will protect you from the attempts of Lord Oakendale as well as assist your inquiries concerning those so deservedly dear to you."

Laura could not find words is sufficient to thank Mrs. Greville for her extreme kindness; and, having exhausted the effusions of her grateful heart, she began asking Mrs. Greville some questions as to what she knew, or had ever heard, relating to Oakendale-Abbey.

"Why," returned Mrs. Greville, "when you named Oakendale-Abbey, as having resided there, I confess I shuddered at the idea; nevertheless I would not have you suppose that I believe in any of the idle reports current in the neighbourhood; for they are carried to a degree of absurdity and superstition beyond all credit. When they tell you of men and women being seen carrying their heads in their hands, and of monstrous eyes looking through the windows flaming with fire, one is more inclined to laugh at such idle tales than to be alarmed by them. But I must own I have long suspected there was some mystery to be unfolded at the Abbey; but of what nature I cannot even guess. The surprising things you witnessed there confirms this belief, and I wish it were seriously investigated.

"It has now many years since I saw the inside of the Abbey; and it was by no means a fit residence for the fair and inhabitant whom I went to visit; it must been now infinitely worse, and a frightful place to send a young person to! I only wonder how you could support yourself under such circumstances, and it is like the rest of Lord Oakendale's conduct."

"My dear Madam," said Laura, "I understand the Abbey had not been inhabited since the memory of any person now living; who then could you go there to visit?"

"Indeed," replied Mrs. Greville, "I ought to explain myself; for what I said must seem as mysterious as any of the stories which are related. I went to see a picture of the present Lord's mother, which, upon some family feuds, was sent down to this Abbey as a punishment, or rather mortification, to the person it represented. It was allowed to be an uncommonly and well finished picture, and was done by an Italian master; and the sweetness of the countenance exceeded any I ever saw, except that I am now beholding!"

Laura bowed her thanks for the compliment, and asked Mrs. Greville "if the picture did not hang in a room which she described; and if it was not in the Van Dyke taste?"

Mrs. Greville replied, "that it was, and was a beautiful full length portrait."

"Yes," said Laura, "it was in that room that I discovered the letter-case; and I can never be persuaded but Eugene must have been in that apartment; for I think (she added, with a sigh) he would not have parted with it to anyone else."

"That is, indeed," said Mrs. Greville, "a very extraordinary circumstance, and which time only can discover, and will, I have no doubt; for depend upon it, my dear, you will live to see the clouds disperse, which at present seem to hang over you; and you will one day meet with the reward your merit deserves.—In the meanwhile make yourself easy under my protection; and wait with patience the will of all that all wise disposer of events, who never deserted the innocent, and who is a Father to the fatherless."

Laura said she had every reason to be grateful to Providence, who had, in so many instances, shewn a manifest interposition in her favour, and never more than by placing her under the protection where she now felt herself so happily situated; and in which secure asylum we will, for the present, leave her, and return to give some account of Lord Oakendale, who on arriving at the Abbey, and finding Laura had escaped, became outrageous, and almost frantic with disappointment.

Mary was interrogated with violence and suspicion, as an accomplice in the plan; but she declared her innocence with so much simplicity, that his lordship's anger at length gave way to belief, and he consented to her entreaties of being sent back again into Wales.

His disappointment added fresh fuel to his passion and his resentment; for he vowed vengeance on the poor devoted Laura, should he ever get her again into his hands, of which he entertained but little doubt; knowing that without either horse or carriage, or any one to assist her, she could not have escaped far from the village; and that by bribes and promises, he should very soon have her again in his power. He determined to sleep that night at the Abbey, in this same bed which had been occupied by Laura and Mary. Another was fitted up in an adjoining room for his servant.

It was the first time in his life he had ever been in the Abbey. He thought it horrible and gloomy; and he would have felt some compassion for Laura, for having been consigned to such a place, had not recent flight steeled his heart with the sentiment, and shut every avenue to pity.

The idea of supernatural appearances had never, since he was a child, disturbed his imagination; he therefore, divested of all fear, composed himself to take a refreshing portion of sleep, in order to be the better enabled to make a more vigilant pursuit after Laura the next day. He had not, however, been in bed two hours before he was very much surprised by a foot-step, and a low murmuring voice, which appear to be not far distant. He called his servant.

The poor man readily obeyed the summons, for he had been equally alarmed. He entered the room pale and trembling, and was going to relate his fears; but Lord Oakendale felt his valour return, and being ashamed to confess his fright to his servant, he only said there were rats in the house; talked loud, blustered, and ordered his servants to return to his bed.

In about an hour the steps and the voice were heard again. The idea that Laura was concealed in some part of the Abbey occurring to his mind, he hastily called up his servant, and ordering him to bring lights, he prepared himself to search the Abbey. The man having heard the report of its being haunted, and being already very much alarmed at what had passed, was not quite so willing to enter into such service, and endeavour to persuade his Lord to wait for the morning; but this suggestion only stimulated Lord Oakendale to begin the search, having worked up his mind to the firm opinion that he should find Laura. They each took a light, and proceeded through all the apartments; Lord Oakendale with his sword drawn in his hand, swearing to murder the first person he found, if they should endeavour to screen Laura from his possession. He likewise exhorted his servant to be courageous, and to follow his example.

The man stood greatly in need of the exhortation; for as he tremblingly led the way, and carried the lights, he expected to lose his senses by the sight of some tremendous apparition; and when Lord Oakendale opened the rusty locks and creaking doors, he thought his heart would have died with in him.

When they approached the room, in which was the trunk and skeleton, Lord Oakendale made a stop.—The gloominess of its appearance, rendered doubly so by the still dark hour of the night, had a momentary effect upon his resolution; but he resumed his courage, and surveyed the room. The servant trembled, and scarcely lifted up his eyes. They approached the trunk wherein the skeleton was deposited. Lord Oakendale ordered his servants to lift up the lid; and the light had no sooner glanced upon the ghastly figure, then the man, dropping the lid from his hand, exclaimed, "God preserve us! here is a dead man, bigger than a giant, with saucer eyes, and huge limbs!"

"Ridiculous!" exclaimed his Lord, at the same moment examining it himself, though not without feeling a chill at this relic of mortality; and he was for a moment undetermined whether or not to proceed, when the idea of Laura again renewed his courage, and he advanced to the cloister, and following the light carried by the terrified servant, arrived at the partition, which presented neither a door, or any means of opening it, whatsoever.

This circumstance strongly excited his curiosity, and this aided by disappointment, brought him to a desperate pitch of resolution; and observing the boards were but thin, he set his whole force against them, and, with a terrible crash, they all at once gave way. A confused rumbling noise assailed his ears; but how were all his senses stiffened with horror at the site of a human body, apparently dead, but sitting upright in a coffin!

Lord Oakendale started at the sight; the sword dropped from his hand, and he stood petrified with terror and amazement. The servant had fallen down, and nearly extinguished the light; and as Lord Oakendale stooped down to preserve it, he fancied a cold hand grasped him. His trembling legs barely supported him from this scene of terror! The servant was nearly deprived of his senses. His master assisted him to rise, and hastily turning towards the cloister, they made the best of their way through the apartments they had before so minutely examined, rushed out of the Abbey, and alarmed the village!

The clock struck four, and some of the peasants were already rising to their work: and seen his Lordship, as they supposed, making his escape from the Abbey, they concluding he had seen something to terrify and alarm him, gathered round, with a hope of being gratified by some marvellous adventure; but his Lordship was in no humour to relate wonders. He ordered horses to the carriage, and getting into it, bestowed something like a curse upon Laura, the Abbey, and all the infernal spirits that inhabit it.

And this disposition he pursued his way to London. Various were his conjectures during his journey; and he could form his idea into no system of probability as to the strange and unaccountable sights he had beheld at the Abbey. He resolved, indeed, to have them thoroughly investigated on some future occasion; but he never intended again to encounter them himself. He suffered great uneasiness on account of Laura. He found he loved her with sincere affection. Her idea dwelt upon his heart with more uneasy sensations than he had ever before experience, and although his love for her was neither founded upon esteem or delicacy. But he was a mere sensualist; yet a something of tender anxiety was combined with his passion for her. "Where could she be, and to what evil and sufferings might she be exposed?"[29] These were intruding questions that forced themselves with compassionate tenderness, upon a heart but little alive to the softer feelings of humanity. In this state we will therefore leave him for the present, in order to give

---

[29] Considering his previous behavior, Lord Oakendale's actions are indeed strange. Is he softening his original horrific plan for Laura? ...or does he simply fear that someone may damage what he considers to be his property?

our readers an account of some other personages who have as yet appeared but in the background of the history.

Lady Oakendale, of whom we have said that she was the only daughter of Lord Westhaven, and that her immense fortune was the only inducement Lord Oakendale had for making her his wife, was, as has been before related, by no means calculated to soothe the brow of care, by which her Lord was now appraised on the contrary, they had conceived an aversion bordering upon hatred for each other. But, in order to elucidate her history, we must go back to a very early period of her life. She was an only child, and had lost her mother when she was very young; and from that circumstance might date all her misfortunes, as she was consigned to the care of a governess, and other mercenary dependents, whose chief object was to inculcate in her the idea of her own consequence, by continually reminding her of her great fortune she would in future process, as well as the higher rank she held in life.[30]

After being taught to possess various accomplishments necessary for her situation, in so superficial manner, that they could neither be an entertainment to others, nor any source to herself, she found a void in her mind, which she would sometimes

---

[30] Inculcate is to teach or impress an idea upon someone by frequent repetition. Apparently Lord Oakendale is attempting to influence Laura's firmly held opinions.

endeavour to fill up by attempts at fancy work, or some ingenious device peculiar to the sex; but on these occasions she was always informed, that such employments were by no means to fit for her to engage in; and that there were people sufficient who would be glad to do such little services for the gratuity which she had it so amply in her power to bestow.

Thus was her mind (perhaps naturally good) withdrawn from every source of instruction or amusement, and left to the idle workings of phantastic conceits, which will always, if not subdued by rational amusements, lead to an indolent lassitude, totally destructive of every moral and social virtue.

As soon as she was of an age to appear at her father's stable, and be introduced by some of his acquaintance to public places, her whole mornings were spent in trying on various caps, and other dresses; consulting her glass, assorting her ribbands and feathers to her complexion, and the colour of her hair. Her person was neither handsome or otherwise; her skin was fair, but her features were irregular and wanted animation; and she had acquired an air of hauteur, which, being unaccompanied by grace, bordered upon ill-humour.

Lord Westhaven, after the death of his wife, grew fond of drinking, and engaged in a dissipated way of life, neither consistent with his age or station. He loved his daughter, as something very nearly allied to himself; but he took no pains to regulate her conduct, or to improve her understanding. He frequently brought men home to dinner, whose free conversation was neither suppressed by her presence, nor regulated by propriety; and from these she heard toasts and sentiments by no means proper for her contemplation; which gave her a bold assurance, but little consistent with the delicacy of the feminine character.

She was known to have an immense fortune, and of course was addressed by every man who wished to advance his own.

An officer in the guards, of the name of Vincent, was the most assiduous in his attentions to her; and, indeed, for a time, kept all the rest at a distance. He had an uncommon fine person, and was sufficiently well skilled in the science of fashion and flattery to render himself agreeable. He studied her disposition with the nicest attention; and, been well aware that her father designed her for a man of rank, having no pretensions of that nature at that time, he was resolved to supplant those that had; he therefore thought he had only to secure her affections as the prelude to the possession of her fortune.

She loved Vincent as a girl of her education and disposition would naturally do, who was captivated by his person, and pleased with his attentions. But she knew he could not introduce her into the rank in life her ambition led her to suppose she must fill, and she could not endure the sound of plain Mrs. Vincent; yet the idea of a tender lover, encouraged in secret, and met by stratagem, enraptured her imagination, and was so consonant to her wishes, that what she first admitted as a charming amusement for her leisure hours, became a serious consideration, and in the end, a source of increasing misery.

It happened about this time that the Earl of Oakendale was introduced to her by her father; and, after a few interviews, she was told to consider him as her lover and destined husband.

Lord Oakendale was a man whom Miss Rainsford might have liked, had not her heart been devoted to Vincent; yet the idea of being a Countess, with all the flattering appendages of a title, gave a preponderancy to the scale of grandeur, and made her accept Lord Oakendale's proposals, and her father's commands, without any seeming reluctance.

Meantime Vincent could not bear to lose the golden prize, and have the mortification to behold, what he had thought so well secured to himself, given to another. Then fired with jealousy, and disappointed in his ambitious views, he meditated mischief and revenge. First he thought to induce her to consent to a clandestine marriage, but the idea that, in case of high resentment from her father, she might, instead of a large portion, not bring him a shilling, proved a too weighty consequence, and he durst not risk such a chance.

The next suggestion was more of a more feasible aspect. Miss Rainsford loved him passionately, though he believed she loves title and splendour better; the only way then to supplant his rival, and secure his interest, was to make marriage with him necessary to save her reputation. There were tender moments, in which Miss Rainsford's prudence might yield to love, and probable consequences might bring even the Earl to solicit a marriage, to which, under no other circumstances, he would have consented.

Having concerted this plan; not indeed the most honourable one, but such as might well be expected from the nature of the parties concerned, he studied, at the next private interview, the most insinuating address, and the most the pathetic complaints. He knew the exact state of Miss Rainsford's heart, and upon what principle all her sentiments were guided. He lamented, in terms of despair, his cruel and unmerited fate; he declared his love was founded upon the noblest basis, that of affection for her alone; whilst Lord Oakendale's was merely for her fortune, without the smallest particle of passion for that enchanting person, which was the sole object of his adoration; yet such was his regard, such his self-denial, that he would renounce all hope, and yield her to his hated rival; whilst he tore himself away, never more to behold her, and sought, in the field of battle, that death which alone could release him from the misery of his present sufferings.

This was a language to persuasive, and too powerful, for the tender feelings of Miss Rainsford. Charmed with such flattering delusions she couldn't refuse nothing to so fond and tender a lover; her melting heart acknowledged all his influence, and she became his mistress. For awhile the stolen enjoyments became sweeter by repetition; but what were the mortifying reflections she underwent, when a short time shewed the effects of their innocent connexion.

This was the boundary of Vincent's wishes, and he concluded his fortune made; yet such was the strange and unnatural disposition of Miss Rainsford, whether ambition got the better of all softer ties, or from what ever cause her mind was influence, she no sooner discovered her situation than she conceived a mortal aversion to the author of her disgrace; and, contrary to all his expectations, and to his utter astonishment, she gave every encouragement to the match with Lord Oakendale. Struck with aversion and disgust to the woman, who could be capable of acting so contrary to delicacy and every feminine virtue, his heart recoiled at the idea of a marriage with her, and he secretly triumphed in the disgrace of his rival.

Meantime some embarrassing circumstances occurred relating to the settlements of estates, and necessarily delayed the match, which Miss Rainsford could not, with propriety, hasten. Her situation, therefore, was become truly dreadful; and before the completion of the settlements, she found herself four months advanced in her pregnancy, by the man whom she had sacrificed to her ambition; and which ambition still urged her to complete the sacrifice by giving her hand at the altar to Lord Oakendale. The consequence of this marriage has before been described.

Driven to the last extremity, within two months of her time, every day making it more difficult to conceal her situation, and finding it impossible, from the date of her marriage to impose the fruit of her guilt upon her Lord, she had recourse to the counsel and opinion of a confidant—the woman who had been her favoured attendant from her youth, and to whose pernicious flattery, and improper advice, she in some degree owed her ruin!

This woman's name was Marcel; she was a native of France and had improved the deceit and hypocrisy of that country by the lowest devices of this; she seemed, however the proper friend, upon this trying emergency. After Lady Oakendale had bribed her to secrecy, she intrusted her with the whole history of her amour; and, having consulted upon the wisest and most prudent methods, she suggested that of retiring into the country, under the pretence of ill health, where she would remain till after her delivery; and this was the more easy to put in practice from the little attention Lord Oakendale had ever shewn to his lady since their marriage; for he seemed never in the smallest degree, interested about any thing she did, nor ever paid the least regard to her health, or any things that concerned her. Thus was she at full liberty to pursue her own plan and inclinations.

Everything therefore was arranged, and she went to a retired village in Buckinghamshire; where, passing for the widow of an officer, she was delivered of a son in the presence of only the accoucheur,[31] and her faithful confidant.

The former had been engaged to secrecy upon his honour, for he was above taking a larger bribed than his fee; and Marcel was to provide a nurse, and entirely undertake the charge of the infant.

The gentleman employed upon this occasion was by nature humane, and from principle generous. Without prying into the reasons which made secrecy necessary, he always wished to witness the effusions of natural affection from the mother to her offspring, under whatsoever circumstances it might be produced; he therefore took the smiling babe to the sight of lady Oakendale, in the hope that its helpless innocence might plead for maternal protection. But no sooner had she cast her eyes upon the unfortunate object of her disgrace, and she gave a shriek of abhorrence, and that he would take the odious brat from her sight!

Shocked at her inhuman exclamation, he tenderly wrapped up the infant, saying, "Poor child! this

---

[31] Someone who assists at a birth—a mid-wife.

unnatural behaviour will lead me to discover the mystery of thy birth; and amply shall thy unfeeling mother provide for thy necessities."

He proved his words; for he made such enquiries as satisfied his curiosity, and justified the measures he took to see that the child was properly nursed; and during its infancy and afterwards, he repeatedly obtained large sums from lady Oakendale for its education; for he made no scruple to inform her ladyship that he knew the whole secret, which he threatened to expose and discover, unless she acquiesced in his demands. In reality he could only guess at the transaction; but at her allowance for pin money was very ample; and he had taken an uncommon fancy to the child, has it advanced in years, he took the entire charge of him, and chose that the boy's education should be upon the most liberal plan.

Nothing was omitted that could improve his capacity, and give him every advantage; and he had attained the age of twenty years, adorned with every grace and accomplishment, which elegance of person and a natural understanding, enlarged by the highest cultivation, could bestow, without ever experiencing one glance of parental favour.

There was no part of his life, in which he had been led to suppose himself the son of this humane guardian of his youth.

After repeated interrogatories to gain the knowledge, to whom he owed his being, Mr. F.— informed him; that he was really ignorant of the name of his father, but he knew his mother, and that some time or other he should be introduced to her. This time was now approaching. Mr. F.— was brother to Monsieur du Frene, to whom he had sent Eugene, in order to make a proficiency in the French language; and likewise to gain that polish so necessary for a finished character, and to which the easy manners of the French nation generally contributed.

The duel, in which he had so unfortunately engaged, together with the tender attachment he had formed with Laura, were improprieties of sufficient magnitude for Mr. F.— to recall him to England; and to take care that none of the many letters, in which he vowed eternal constancy to Laura should ever be forwarded from England. If, in this instance, Mr. F. — should be blamed for duplicity and unjust dealing, it must be allowed in his favour, that he considered Eugene as a pledge of honour, for whose conduct he must one day be accountable. He had stolen him from his nurse at a very early age, and secreted him from Lady Oakendale and Marcel, in order to restore him as a polished gem when the time arrived, that his virtues should be rendered conspicuous.

Had Eugene fallen in love with any other than an adopted child of his brothers, he would have let the progress of their attachment taken its course; as it was, his conscience would not allow of Eugene's forming a connexion, which he considered far beneath his birth, until he had been properly acknowledged by those to whom he was united by the dearest ties.

Lady Oakendale, from the hour of her marriage, had never experienced a moment of felicity, except that which he she derived from a round of dissipation, and a moving in a vortex of fashion. Her Lord never cared for her. The fortunate she had brought him was the only inducement he ever had for making her his wife; and neither of them had endeavoured to render the marriage state happy, by any attempts to please the other.

Lady Oakendale had, soon after her marriage, the mortification to hear that Captain Vincent had succeeded to a title and estate, by the unexpected death of a distant relation. He was now Edward Lord Vincent of Vincent Castle, in the kingdom of Ireland. He had been twice married; but had no children by either of his wives, and the title and estate at his death would descend to a very distant branch, if he left no heir; but he had a power of appointing a successor to his estate, though not to his title.

The fruit of his intrigue with Lady Oakendale often occured to his remembrance. He had never made any inquiries of her ladyship concerning it; and she, on account of her having the secret profoundly observed, had carefully kept him from every information concerning the event. Lord Vincent, now wishing more than ever to know if he was a father, and feeling the necessity of appointing an heir to his vast fortune, caused an indirect application to be made to her ladyship concerning his offspring, and to know if it now existed.

Alarmed at this unexpected demand, and terrified lest the secret should be discovered, she instantly sent for Mr. F.—, desiring him to conceal, as far as possible, the son she knew he had taken under his care, as it was now become a matter of the utmost importance to her, that his birth should be buried in oblivion; and as she had assured Lord Vincent that the child had died in its infancy, it became necessary to engage Mr. F— to corroborate the falsehood.

Having, therefore, explained her motives, Mr. F.— found this was the moment of discovery for which he had so long wished and was likely to be fortunate for his young favourite; he therefore determined to dissemble and acquiesce in her demands till he had gained the wished for intelligence; he therefore told her ladyship, that it entirely depended upon herself to secure his confidence, by informing him, without reserve, who was the real father of that son, whose future concealment alone depended upon a true information.

She at first resolutely refuse to make the discovery; he knowing it would be in vain to entreat, or to urge any plea of the injustice she was doing her son, or to address her tender feelings, he only peremptorily insisted upon knowing the truth, as the only terms upon which he would keep the secret.

After a very long and obstinate resistance, and making the future concealment of her son the condition of her confession, she informed him, that Lord Vincent was Eugene's father.

Mr. F.— was elated with pleasure at the prospect of seeing the noble youth, the darling of his hopes, so happily placed; and, instead of venturing to let him remain where he then was, in another kingdom, he immediately sent for him home, determined to keep him under his own eye till the time arrived when he should introduce him to his father, lest the machinations of Lady Oakendale might frustrate his design. Nor were these apprehensions needless; for her ladyship having informed her faithful confidant of the result of Mr. F.—'s business, this artful woman instantly foresaw the consequences, and begged her ladyship, as she valued her reputation and peace of mind, to counteract the designs of Mr. F.—; which she thought might easily be contrived, by demanding to have an interview with her son, in which Mr. F.— might be present when her ladyship should affect so much fondness for her son, that Mr. F.— might be so effectually deceived, that he would be induced to intrust him to her care; after which she would engage to have him concealed.

Meantime Mr. F.— recalled Eugene from France, and it seemed now a proper time to introduce him to his mother. In consequence of this plan, so coincident with theirs, and so well calculated to facilitate the designs of

Marcel, Eugene was accordingly introduced to his mother in the presence of Mr. F.—; who, partial, in the highest degree, to the young man, could not suppose, but when a mother beheld the offspring of her fondest love in the person of one of the finest figures, nature ever formed, and animated of the most interesting countenance that could adorn the human frame, her heart would undergo a change of sentiment, and a thousand tender nameless sensations would betray the feelings of a mother. Nor was he quite mistaken. Lady Oakendale, depraved as she was, could not behold the captivating figure and manly beauty of his features, softened to a tenderness of expression at being in the presence of a parent, without emotions to which she had before been a stranger; and when he threw himself at her feet, with the most affectionate duty, a tear stole down her cheek; and, pressing him to her bosom, she had no occasion to have recourse to dissimulation to impress the maternal embrace.

Her trembling voice could scarce articulate a sentence, and she would have continued holding him to her heart, till the callous texture had been softened to the most virtuous sensibility, had she not been recalled to recollection by the interposition of Marcel; who, observing the soft sensations which the sight of her son had inspired, reminded her of the dangerous consequences that might attend her giving way to them;

the lady Oakendale instantly resumed her composure, and steadily preserved her purpose.

Mr. F.— saw that she had been seriously affected, and the sight gave him infinite satisfaction; but he could not entirely rely upon a character like hers, and happily suspecting that she was, in some degree, acting a part, he would not therefore be persuaded to leave Eugene with her; but promising she should soon be indulged with another interview, he took him away, and lost no time in preparing his mind to expect the embraces of a father also, although he did not yet think proper to inform him who he was.

Lord Vincent was now in Ireland, and Mr. F.— impatiently waited his return to England, when he would restore him a son every way worthy the honours of his house and name; and from whom he expected Eugene would meet with a more sincere reception than he had received from his mother. He was at the same time particularly cautious to conceal the Eugene, as much as possible from the knowledge of Lady Oakendale, till the time came when he should be safe under the protection of Lord Vincent.

The lively disposition of Eugene could to but ill brook the restraints imposed upon him by Mr. F. —, and could not conceive any danger should arise from his going whithersoever his fancy led him.

He had one night been at Ranelagh, in order to amuse his mind, which became oppressed in the extreme, on account of never hearing anything of his beloved Laura. He had written letter after letter, fraught with the tenderest expressions of regard, and everlasting constancy, all of which were intercepted by Mr. F.—, for the reasons heretofore mentioned.

The horrid accounts every day received from Paris, filled his mind with the utmost cruel apprehensions; and, although he tried to divert his fears from so melancholy a subject, by frequently running to places of public resort; yet he always returned with a double portion of wretchedness, as they only recalled back the remembrance of similar scenes past with his beloved Laura.

When he returned from Ranelagh the above mentioned evening, he was happy more than usual. He told Mr. F.— he had been in company with a gentleman who had given him so charming a description of the Lakes in Westmoreland and Cumberland, that if anything could remove his melancholy, and divert his imagination, it would be a visit to those celebrated Lakes, and to rambling about that romantic and delightful country. Mr. F.— thinking he might in such an excursion, be more out of the reach and power of Lady Oakendale, than he was by staying in London, thought it best to make no opposition to his request; and Eugene, therefore, obtained leave to make a tour to the northern part of England, where, he said, he should find some young friends, with whom he had formed an intimacy at school. Mr. F.— could not refuse so reasonable a request, and imprudently suffered him to departure without any attendant.

Having promised to write very frequently, Eugene took an affectionate leave of Mr. F.—, with no other weight upon his mind than that which arose from his being ignorant of the state of Laura.

After a fortnight had elapsed, and Mr. F.— had heard not from Eugene, he began to be alarmed. He took every method in his power to gain intelligence of him, but without effect. His mind underwent a tormenting suspense, for he really loved him like a son; and, although he did not chuse to inform lady Oakendale whither he was gone; yet such were his suspicions of her, that he caused such an application to be made to her as he thought might bring him some information; but all it no purpose; she pleaded ignorance of his destination and pretended great concern at the circumstance.

Mr. F.— suffered the most poignant grief; he accused himself for allowing him to depart alone, and on this score he endured many bitter reflections.

As time wore away, the sweet hope of presenting a wished for son to a fond father, which son justified by his merit and accomplishments, and even exceeded the most sanguine hopes of the most partial parents; these hopes, and flattering ideas, at length gave placed to the bitter remembrance of the loss each had sustained.

The continual advertisements he caused to be inserted in the daily papers, besides hand-bills, and every other inquiry which could lead to a discovery, were ineffectually continued for many months, without bringing him the smallest information, or clue, to recover his favourite.

Fatigued with repeated disappointments and not knowing what further methods to pursue, he waited upon Lord Vincent, the first hour he heard he was arrived in England, informing that nobleman that he was a father; but that his mind was torn with perplexity as to the present existence of that son, on whose virtues and accomplishments Mr. F.- expatiated with the fond partiality of a parent.

Lord Vincent felt a glow of parental affection rise in his bosom, which was every moment increased on the recital of his merits, and soon occasioned and impatient desire of beholding him.

When Mr. F.— mentioned his recent loss, Lord Vincent was firmly persuaded that lady Oakendale was privy to the concealment; particularly when Mr. F.— informed him, that he suffered Eugene to go alone; and that he had since his departure, discovered that he had a private interview with lady Oakendale the night before he set out upon his tour, and informed her to what part of England he was going to make his excursion.

Persuaded in this opinion, they debated upon that the measures to be pursued, which would be most likely to bring her ladyship to make the discovery. They agree to begin by gentle methods, and treating her by the most friendly and secret persuasions; and if this failed, to make more decided and arbitrary conditions.

In the meantime, and during these negociations, Lord Oakendale's mind suffered so much painful uneasiness, as to produce a slow fever; he felt a cruel disappointment at the loss of Laura, for whom he had conceived the most ardent affection; and the manner of her disappearance, together with the dreadful and unaccountable phantoms at the Abbey, had so much agitated his imagination, that it was sometime before he could bring his reason to that state of composure, which was necessary in the projecting a scheme he had planned for investigating the horrors which had so imposed upon his understanding at the Abbey.

He had formed and rejected many designs for this purpose, when Lady Oakendale, before he adopted any, was seized with a violent illness; the consequence, (as Mr. F.— supposed) of the negociation between her and Lord Vincent, concerning the concealment of Eugene.

Lord Oakendale seldom gave himself much trouble about her, and her indispositions were as little regard as herself; but this became of a very serious nature; and, upon his lordship's being desired to attend her sick bedchamber, he obeyed the summons with unusual alacrity, secretly hoping that he should not only be released from a bondage, from which he had never derived the smallest comfort or satisfaction; but should yet be honorably blessed with the hand of his charming Laura, could she ever again be discovered.

Elated with these hopes, he hastened to her apartment with no unpleasing ideas; and, throwing and artful dejection into his countenance, he was approaching her bed with a tender expression of enquiry; when he started, and was diverted from his purpose by the surprise of beholding her with Lord Vincent on one side of the bed, and Mr. F.— on the other, attended by a gentleman of the law taking notes from her confession.

The moment she beheld Lord Oakendale she ceased speaking. Her eye-lids fell, a sudden convulsion affected her articulation, and she had only time to pronounce, in a trembling voice, and disjointed words, "My — son! — Oakendale Abbey."—When she sunk down and expired!

Lord Oakendale, much as he had wished for her death, was shocked at its sudden approach; and, not being able to comprehend the scene before him, and still more astonished at her naming a son, together with the Oakendale Abbey, he demanded of her faithful confidently, Marcel, "who was in the room?"

"Why, Lord Vincent, and the other gentleman, were present?"

"And if her lady was in her right senses when she talked of a son, and Oakendale Abbey?"

The confusion of the scene, and the sudden dissolution of lady Oakendale, prevented every one present from giving an immediate answer; and Mr. F.— seeing Marcel instantly about to quit the room, instead of answering the interrogatory of Lord Oakendale, he eagerly seized her arm, and leading her up to his lordship, said, "there is much to be explained, my Lord, and I look upon this woman to be able to give the clearest account of the mystery which yet remains unfolded; for this reason it seems proper to have her secured."

Lord Vincent joined in this proposition; and having collected proper assistance for the security of Marcel, the rest of the party left the room of the deceased, and were joined by the gentlemen of the law, who preceded to read the minutes he had taken from her ladyship's dying confession. They consisted of a faithful relation of her being four months advanced in her pregnancy by Edward Vincent, then an officer in the guards at the time she was married to Lord Oakendale.

That finding it impossible to impose upon his lordship, by pretending the child to be his, she confided her secrets to Marcel; by whose contrivance she was in five months after her marriage delivered of a son at — in Buckinghamshire.

That this was managed the more easily, on account of the terms upon which she lived with her Lord.

That Marcel had engaged to secrete the child, and keep it at nurse, which she did, at a very little expense, till the end of five years; when the woman, who had taken the charge of it told them "that he had been stolen from her."

That this circumstance gave them no great uneasiness till about three years after, when Mr. F.— declared himself to have been the person who had taken the child away, and from that time made large demands upon her for its education, always threatening her with a discovery in case of non-compliance.

That within the last two years Mr. F.— had insisted upon her seeing the young man, and extorted a confession from her of his real father, to which, after great reluctance, she yielded, and consented to see her son. She confessed, that the interview made her feel herself a mother; but the idea of his being introduced into the world as the son and heir of Lord Vincent, filled her with perpetual alarm of a discovery, and made her suppress all her tender feelings, and again have recourse to Marcel, to continue some method of securing the preservation of her fame, before Lord Vincent made a public acknowledgment of him as his son. Various methods were suggested; but none seemed proper to adopt, till the idea of travelling alone was artfully contrived to allure him from a Mr. F.—; and the gentlemen, who met him at Ranelagh, was by them engaged for the purpose of facilitating their design; and having so ordered that his curiosity should be excited by the accounts of Oakendale Abbey, he was there entrapped, and secured in a subterraneous part of it, where to the best of her knowledge, he now remained.

This was the substance of lady Oakendale's confession; and an oath of confirmation was administered to her by the gentlemen of the law, who was also a justice of the peace. She found, however, her mind was not relieved by the confession, unless Lord Oakendale was made acquainted with her guilt, and would pronounce her pardon; and, being sensible that the hour was approaching, when the most ample confession would not lessen her crimes whilst one particle of dissimulation remained, she begged to see Lord Oakendale, declaring her intention of acknowledging her deception, and imploring his pardon; but the design was sufficient, and we hope accepted; she was, therefore spared the confusion of confessing to him, whom she had most injured, by the Minister of Death, who, on the moment of Lord Oakendale's approach, prevented her adding more than the above mentioned words.

Having recovered their surprise and given the necessary orders for the interment of her ladyship, Lord Oakendale was equally desirous with Lord Vincent to make the investigation of Oakendale Abbey. He had no doubt but Laura had been entrapped, as well as Eugene; and the impatient desire he had of making her his wife, increased his anxiety, and even possessed him with the torments of jealousy, last Eugene, being in similar circumstances with herself, might be captivated with her charms, and endeavour to make his escape and with her. Stimulated with ideas of this nature, his mind was kept in a perpetual agitation, and his impatience would scarcely allow time for the necessary preparations to be made for the journey, and to collect proper persons for so arduous an undertaking.

Marcel would not, or could not, give them any more information than what has been already related. She declared she had never seen Oakendale Abbey, although she had reason to believe that Eugene was at this time conceal there; she was however, kept in close custody.

Lord Oakendale determined, that if Laura was found, no forms of ceremony should for an hour retard his marriage with her. He considered the confession Lady Oakendale had made of her duplicity and infidelity a sufficient release from the marriage covenant; and which gave him full liberty to form a second union, long before the usual time of mourning was expired for the first. It was not to be supposed he should be upon any terms of great cordiality with Lord Vincent; yet, as the present case made him as interested a person as himself in the projected discovery, he allowed himself to waive all animosity for the present, and to confide with Lord Vincent upon the plan of operation necessary to be made upon the occasion.

At length the arrangements were all adjusted, and a chosen sets were appointed to accompany the two Lord's, Mr. F.— and the lawyer, into Cumberland, in order to discover both Eugene and Laura, and to erase the Abbey to the ground, if it was necessary to facilitate the search.

Lord Oakendale was elated with hope, and would allowed no suggestion to intrude that bore the most distant idea to any circumstance that was not consonant to his wishes. Laura, the charming Laura, should now be lady Oakendale, and put in immediate possession of all his wealth. Fancy had painted her with additional allurements and her having been so long confined in a subterraneous abode, would render her more alive to freedom, and grateful for his splendid offers. With these flattering hopes he endeavoured to beguile the tedious hours that intervened before the time fixed for their departure.

On the evening of the day before they were to begin their journey, he was indulging in one of the above delightful reveries, when a servant opened the door of his library, and informed him that a gentleman wished to speak with him upon business of importance, which could not be trusted to a messenger.

Lord Oakendale peevishly ordered him to be admitted, at the same time determining that no business whatsoever should location a delay to their projected expedition. Accordingly a middle aged clergyman was ushered into the room, and after that usual compliments had passed, he asked Lord Oakendale "if he had any relation in the East-Indies?"

Lord Oakendale replied, "yes, he had once a brother, whom, he believed, was slain in battle in the East-Indies."

The gentleman whose name was Martin, then proceeded to inform his lordship, "that a few weeks since he was called upon to attend one of his dying parishioners, whose conscience seemed to labour under some very heavy oppression; and who said he had been on board a ship coming to England from the East-Indies, when she was taken by a French privateer. That there were several passengers on board, amongst whom was a little girl, who had a small bag of quilted satin tied round her neck, which she always held with great care, and consequently he supposed to contain something valuable. Indeed, he heard one of the women on board say that it did, and caution the child not to part with it. That he had frequently meditated to get it from her, but never had an opportunity till the day they were taken to the prison in Paris; when, seeing one of the French soldiers tearing it from the neck of the child, he persuaded him that it's was only charm against infection;[32] and, by making some trifling exchange, secured the bag for his own. Upon opening it, he found it contained some jewels of value,

---

[32] Even as late as the end of the 18th Century, the plague of the 1300's was a constant fear. It was believed that charms would word off infection and the plague. Many believed that wormwood, sown into a pouch, or used to fumigate the home, could keep the plague away while others wore amulets around their necks made of saints' portraits, seeds, and other charms which were folded inside of a Latin prayer script.

carefully concealed, by being quilted between the satin. There was likewise a miniature picture of an officer, and a written paper, signifying to the child was. The picture and the paper he preserved; but the jewels he sold, and found the money amounted to some hundred pounds.

The picture and the paper he always wished to have restored to their right owners, and, upon the exchange of prisoners, he made some enquiry after the relations of the child; but, finding they were persons of consequence, he was afraid to make any application to them, lest it might lead to a discovery of the theft. The time he said it was now come, when he would give worlds never to have had them in his possession; nor could he recollect one single satisfaction or pleasure that the money for which the jewels sold had given him; that he sincerely repented having wronged the child; that he begged I would pray to God to forgive him; and all the restitution he could now make, was to place the picture and the paper in my hands, beseeching me, if possible, to find out to the child, or its relations, and to restore what yet remained of their property. He added, that he had lately met with a woman who had been taken prisoner with the child, and he said it had been put on board, and intrusted to her care by a female Negro, who had lived with its parents; and that the child was carried from the prison by a surgeon, of the name of du Frene, who attended them. Mr. Martin having finished his relation, Lord Oakendale tremblingly opened the paper. The first thing that struck his sight was the picture of his brother; that brother upon whom he had bestowed so little care or anxiety, and whose exact resemblance, now before his eyes, recalled to his recollection his many virtues, and filled his heart with remorse and regret that he had so cruelly neglected them, and paid so little regard to his memory. Having paid this late tribute of affection, he proceeded to open the paper, which contained the following lines, written in his brother's own hand:

"Laura Carleton, daughter of William Carleton, and Zelima his wife; was born at Madras, April the 14th, 1778, and is the only surviving heir of the Oakendale family.

"William Carleton."

"This paper, picture and jewels, are the property of Laura Carleton."

No sooner had Lord Oakendale read this paper than the colour forsook his cheeks; his eyes glistened, and he held the paper in his trembling hand, while he preserved a profound silence. A flash of conviction rushed upon his mind that Laura might be, and was in all probability his own niece; that Laura, whom he was upon the point of making his wife. He hesitated for a few seconds in the faint hope that some mistake might prove the matter to be different; but the circumstances were too strong to admit of any doubt; and however he might wish to disbelieve the facts, and impulse of a difference nature from what he had hitherto experienced, made him shudder for his own crimes, at the same time that he felt an uncommon interest in the state of Laura.

He again looked at his brother's picture: again he examined the hand writing: it was certainly his brother's, for it was a remarkable hand; and again it recalled to his remembrance the thousand virtues which had marked his character, and the little value that had been placed upon them by those who stood in the nearest relation to him. Should Laura really be his niece, and the only surviving branch of the house of Oakendale, with what pleasure should he allow her the possession of that fortune, to which she derived as much claim from her virtues, as from hereditary right!

Such are the ties of nature, that his pride exulted in calling that a woman niece, whom he had a short time before designed and solicited for prostitution.—During the time these reflections were passing in his mind, he sat musing up without muttering a word: but at last recollecting Mr. Martin, he thanked him with unfeigned sincerity, and told him he had every reason to believe that he had seen the person, whom exactly answered that description of the child, and who he had no doubt was his niece.

He then proceeded to thank Mr. Martin for the trouble he had taken to convey the information to him: and, without telling him by what means she came there, he added, that he verily believed she was at this time concealed in an interior part of an old Abbey belonging to himself in Cumberland. That the next morning had been fixed for their journey there, to make an enquiry which the present information he had received would greatly accelerate.

Mr. Martin congratulated Lord Oakendale on the prospect of finding his niece; and here it may not seem improper to give our readers a more particular account of Laura's father in order more clearly to elucidate the identity of her birth.

We have already mentioned that Captain William Carleton embarked with his regiment for the East Indies.

After being driven by contrary winds, they found themselves chased by an Algerian Corsair.[33]

The spirit of the English determined to stand an engagement, in which they were victorious, and very soon boarded the Corsair. On her way to Sallee, to pay the ransom of her brother, who was a captive, there was a Greek Lady, of illustrious birth, and exquisite beauty, and with her four female attendants, who were taken prisoners. The gallantry of the English officers was exerted in acts of attention and consolation to the fair Greeks, who, together with the riches of the cargo made it a prize worthy the bravery of their nation.

The beauty of the chief captive whose name was Zemprenia was the subject of universal admiration, and the captain of the vessel appropriated to her his cabin,

---

[33] A Corsair is a pirate who operated with a governmental commission.

and gave her every accommodation that could render her situation such as to make her forget she was his prisoner: yet nothing could lessen or soothe her affliction: she wept incessantly, and every effort of attention was only answered by the most heart-rendering sighs and laminations: one of her attendance, about the age of sixteen, appeared the least unhappy. Her bewitching smiles, and captivating graces, fascinated the heart of William Carleton; a slight wound he had received in the engagement seemed to excite all her pity, and several tender glances had betrayed a reciprocal passion.

If the elegant person and accomplishments of William had attracted the admiration of Zelima, he was no less enamoured of the fair Greek. She learned his language with facility; but in that of love she was still a greater proficient: and, by the time they arrived at the port of Grand Canary, where they were to release the lady and her attendants, Zelima's heart was not less wounded than her lover's at the cruel idea of separation. She was charmed with all that he possessed. Her religion, her country, and her laws, were all sacrificed to the powerful passion of love; and an English priest, then residing at the port, tied the in dissolvable knot.

She took leave of her mistress Zemprenia with the regret, but not with reluctance; all her duty, love and obedience, were alone due to her husband; and she attended her beloved William to the East, where her tender affection, and unremitting attention, rendered him the happiest of men.

He wrote to Lord Oakendale an account of his marriage with the fair Grecian, and anticipated the pleasure he should derive from presenting this lovely creature to his brother and sister, when the conclusion of war should allow him to return to England; but Lord Oakendale made his marrying a servant a pretence for never answering any of his letters; and three years after, when the Honourable William Carleton's name appeared in the list of those that were killed in battle, Lord Oakendale's heart only palpitated with joy, that the many virtues, and universal good character of his brother, would no longer upbraid, and be a restraint upon his own vices. He put on the exterior of mourning; but he made no sort of inquiry after the widow of William Carleton, or wish to hear that he had left an inheritor to his many virtues.

Thus were the ties of blood dissolved, and a deserted orphan left to seek that protection from strangers which she had a right to claim from relations so near to her. William Carleton had been a bad economist; he had a small younger brother's fortune, and his generous heart was too compassionate, and too liberal, to his fellow creatures, to allow him to be affluent. He was, indeed, too much engaged with his present felicity to make provision for future misfortune, and he was killed by a random shot in the moment of victory!

The fatal wound which deprived him of life was rendered still more poignant by the reflection of leaving Zelima but ill-provided for. She, indeed, did not experience the want of his attention; for no sooner were the fatal tidings brought her of William's death, then her heart sickened, and she only survived to cast a mournful look upon the mangled corpse of her husband, gave a compulsive shriek, and expired, leaving a female infant "unpitied, and forlorn!"

Lord Oakendale threw off all remembrance of his brother with his mourning, and from that time never thought more of the connexion. He followed his pleasures with unremitting avidity, till after the course of a few years, when his constitution began to warn him by frequent intimations that the career, in which he was so deeply engaged, would someday be interrupted.

In these moments of admonition he wished for he knew not what comforts and resources; real friends he had none. The tender endearments of a family he had never known, and his heartfelt and aching void for those dear attentions and solicitudes, which can only be experienced from the tenderest ties.

In these irksome hours, the death of Lady Oakendale was his ultimate wish, and opened to his fancy an inviting path, when he might be at liberty to marry some beautiful young creature, without fortune, whose gratitude would secure to him her affections, and whose youth and health would add herself to his possessions.

But at the time these wishes were formed his hopes were vain for Lady Oakendale was by them no means likely to give him such a chance. Her health was her first care, and, to an excellent constitution she added the most studious attention to its preservation, living by rule, and studying the whole vocabulary of wholesomeness. Neither did her present conduct afford him any hope of breaking the marriage fetters; for amidst the few other virtues she did possess, she adhered strictly to that of chastity, allowing no kind of mercy to those who had been only suspected to have violated the marriage vow.

Such were Lord and Lady Oakendale; when the former, finding his life every day more unhappy, and viewing the infirmities of old age at no great distance from him, he endeavoured to beguile the tedious length of the summer-days, by visiting different water places, which were situated in the most unfrequented and obscure parts of England, where he went by another name, in order to follow his favourite propensities; so that, when he returned to London, and again assumed his name and character as a Senator, he might condemn those vices he had not only been practicing himself, but seducing the innocent and unwary to fall into.

It was during the last summer that he had made an excursion to an interior part of South Wales; from whence his fancy led him to Milford-Haven, where, as he was one evening strolling near the sea, he accidentally met with Laura, the uncommon charms of whose person attracted his notice, and he soon formed a plan of becoming acquainted with her, which succeeding, he in a short time, found himself violently attached.

Her beauty was the least of her merit, and a certain refinement and delicacy which pervaded her whole manner, checked the licentious impulses which the charms of her person occasioned, and he found it necessary to be more upon his guard, and to act with more circumspection in the present case, then any he had ever before encountered.

Her sensible conversation, the observations she made upon the world, as far as she had seen it, would have made her an entertaining companion, had no other charms captivated his senses; but, alluring as she was both in mind and person, he found it impossible to resist so engaging an object, he therefore discovered as much as he could of her story, and found her chief misfortune, and which she most lamented, was the loss of a lady who had brought her up, and from whom she was divided in her passage from France.

Having gathered thus much from her own account, he concluded she was the natural daughter of Monsieur du Frene, who had presented her to his wife as a foundling; that Monsieur was dead, and in all probability she would never again see Madame.

From these circumstances he considered her as a lawful prize for him, and would have immediately offered her settlement as a mistress, had not a certain dignity, and modest superiority in her manner, awed his freedom, and prevented his making such a proposal. He was, however, determined not to lose her, and therefore formed the plan of enticing her to London, under pretence of placing her with a sister till she should discover Madame du Frene.

His insinuating manners and address soon gained upon the unsuspicious heart of Laura; she considered him as old enough to be her father; but for that reason he was still better calculated to be her friend, and she was charmed with the proposal of placing her with his sister. She felt veneration and esteem for Mr. Thoranby (the name he had assumed) and it was not till she arrived in London that she discovered the whole of his deception, which, when he endeavoured to palliate an excuse by pleasing the most ardent love, she solemnly vowed to sacrifice her life to her honour; and, as we have before observed, he sent her to Oakendale Abbey, in hopes that the solitude of the place would induce her to lend a more favourable ear to his wishes.

How did the retrospection of this part of his conduct now fill the mind of Lord Oakendale with corroding thoughts! A ray of gratitude to the Supreme Ruler of all events, who had not permitted him to commit a crime at which his soul shuttered, diffused over him sensations to which he had hitherto been a stranger. He made an ample confession to Mr. Martin of all his conduct, and lamented his errors in such terms of contrition and penitence, that Mr. Martin gave him all possible consolation, and readily joined the party, who were waiting to make the projected search at Oakendale Abbey; to which place their journey was completed as expeditiously as possible.

On their arrival at Oakendale, every thing remained in the state they had left it; and no vestige of any human being appeared to have traversed its gloomy apartments. They proceeded to the room which had, on more occasions than one, caused so much terror, being now a very strong party, properly armed, and every way determined to investigate the mystery.

Lord Oakendale himself led the way. The virtuous principle upon which he now searched for Laura, actuated his mind with a manly resolution; and he felt none of those perturbed tremblings which had assailed his heart on a former occasion.

In one hand he firmly grasped a pistol, in the other a short sword; and having excited his attendance boldly to follow his example, whatever they might encounter, he proceeded into the cloister.

All was still and silent and by force they made their way into the room which terminated it, it was totally dark, and they were obliged to light their candles before they could even distinguish each other!

As soon as they were assisted by the lights, they perceived that the windows, through which very little light could have been admitted, were entirely stopped up, and this seemed to have been done very lately.

Lord Oakendale was convinced it was the very same apartment he had been in before; but everything now bore a different aspect! Nothing appeared in the room but a large table, and some loose boards. There are were evident marks of blood upon many parts of the floor, and in one corner lay a human scull! Lord Oakendale shuddered! The idea of Laura and murder trembled in his heart; at the same time that it renewed his courage, and animated his pursuit. "We will proceed," said he, "and investigate this accursed mystery, or die in the attempt."

"The scull cannot be Laura's" said Mr. F.—; "it could not have been in this state from the time of she has been missing;" yet it might be Eugene and the thought rested upon his imagination with a sickening horror!

Lord Oakendale, having searched every part of the room to no purpose, ordered the floor to be taken up; when, as the men were beginning to execute his orders, they discovered a trap-door, which was instantly opened, and they descended down several winding steps into a huge vault, which seemed to extend under the church. They lighted more candles, and left no part unsearched. No object presented itself; but they picked up bones and sculls in various parts of the vault.

Lord Oakendale fired his pistol; nothing returned but the vibration of its sound; after which a perfect stillness was observed, and a deep hollow groan arrested the ears at every one present. They turned to the left, from whence the sound of the groan proceeded, and perceiving a hollow arch they advanced towards it; but could only be admitted singly, as the sides were too close, and the roof too low to stand upright in.

Lord Oakendale still led the way, and the rest followed. He had again charged his pistol, and carried his sword and a candle in the other hand.

Having advanced several paces, something was thrown in his eyes by an invisible hand, and for a moment he was in total darkness! He again fired his pistol; and as soon as the sound ceased, a faint voice exclaimed, "Oh God, my deliverance is at hand!" The rest of the lights came up, and discovered a hideous figure of a man, with an uplifted bar of iron in his hand ready to strike a fatal blow on the first person who advanced. He was instantly seized, and made it to deliver the keys of a grate which opened to a very small room.

Having secured the man, and entered the prison, in one corner of it appeared an emaciated figure, altered indeed; but in whose thin and pallid countenance Mr. F.— instantly recognized the features of his dear Eugene! He flew to embrace and to present him to Lord Vincent;

whilst Lord Oakendale felt himself disappointed, and involuntarily exclaimed, "Where is my Laura!"

At the name of Laura, Eugene, whom the surprise and the joy of the scene had till then rendered speechless replied, "Laura! What Laura! can she be in this place of horror?"

"There is no time for explanation," said Mr. F.—, "let us return to the less gloomy parts of the Abbey; and as the man, who guarded this infernal dungeon, is secured we may probably force him to a confession of what we still further wish to know; in the meantime let us, my dear boy, give you all the assistance in our power; and revive you by some immediate refreshment."

Eugene, altered and oppressed by the cruel confinement he had so long suffered appeared scarcely the same; yet still a smile of grateful acknowledgment to those who had so unexpectedly procured his enlargement, prejudiced them all in his favour; and the prospect of liberty, together with the joy of beholding the faces of those whom he knew to be his friends, animated his eyes, and gave a glow to his pale cheeks.

Lord Vincent pressed him to his bosom, and acknowledged him for his son; and, although his whole appearance bore testimony to his wretched condition, yet an open countenance, and manly deportment, distinguished the graces of his person, and his sentiments, such as he was able to express, did credit to,

and confirm the education which the good Mr. F. — had
bestowed on him.

Being returned to the other apartments, Lord
Oakendale asked Eugene, in a melancholy tone of voice,
"if he had, during his confinement, ever seen or heard of
a young lady in the Abbey?"

Eugene replied "that he had not." He said, "on the
day he had gained the keys of the Abbey, he thought to
amuse himself with observing the structure of the rooms,
without supposing that any human beings, besides
himself were with inside of it. The inhabitants of the
Oakendale, and particularly the man from whom he had
the keys, had told him of ghosts and spectres;—but this
made him only the more eager to reconnoitre the place;
and not being the least apprehensive of any supernatural
causes, he fearlessly walked about the rooms, in which he
saw nothing either to engage his attention, or excite his
fears; till at last coming into one of the rooms on the first
floor, he was attracted by a portrait, not in very good
preservation, but whose features and countenance bore so
striking a resemblance to Laura, that he was fixed to the
spot, and stood gazing at it with surprise and admiration.

"He had just taken from his pocket a small letter-
case, in which was a little sketch he had himself
attempted upon velium,[34] of the sweetest features in the
world; and was examining and comparing the likeness,

---

[34] A thin, almost see through paper, or a small ceramic tablet.

when he heard footsteps, and instantly found himself pinioned down and secured. All resistance was in vain, and he was harried down to the corrected room in the vault from whence they had now so happily released him; and where he was only supplied with common necessaries, debarred of light, and every social comfort.

"He had" he said, "during his confinement, seen many different faces in the persons who guarded him, and brought his provisions, and each were uniformly silent to the questions he constantly put, in order to gain information of the place he was in, and their designs. Once he had attempted to escape, but was only more closely guarded afterwards. He had heard strange noises, and had reason to believe that some secret practices were carried on in the Abbey; but of what nature he could not give the most distant guess. His spirits had sank to a degree of wretchedness passed all description at the idea of never gaining his liberty, and his mind had given way to the most cruel despair, when he was roused only to a kind of callous indifference upon the report of the first pistol; but when he heard the second fired, and saw through the grated that the guard was agitated, and gathered up the dust to throw at some object which appeared with a light, he felt a ray of comfort to which he had long been a stranger, and which he had so joyfully experienced by his enlargement."

The next step was to interrogate the guard, who, after an obstinate silence, said, "That he was hired for the purpose of guarding the grate, and was relieved in the office by another, who was somewhere about the Abbey." But, after many promises and threatenings of future rewards and punishments, and, after having absolutely disclaimed the knowledge of any other person being confined in the Abbey, he confessed, "he had been hired by a set of people, whose business it was to steal dead bodies, and bring them to the Abbey for dissection;[35] that there was a private door from the church-yard into

---

[35] During the 18th and 19th centuries, as biological sciences and medical disciplines where advancing at a rapid rate, anatomical studies where becoming more important; thus, there was a need for fresh cadavers. Bodies were difficult to come by. Dissection, viewed as an act of damnation, was only legally performed upon executed criminals. A gruesome career developed to supply this demand for fresh corpses: resurrection men, or sack-em-ups. These men would raid freshly buried graves and sell the corpse to local hospitals and medical students for dissection, sometimes charging by the foot. Bodies were not considered anyone's property—so it was not a criminal act in the late 18th century. (However, all grave shrouds were left in the casket - stealing the clothing was considered a crime). The preferred method of grave robbing was to dig a small hole at the head of the fresh grave, about one square foot. After breaking through the casket, a hook was inserted through the soft spot just above the jaw and the body was yanked out of the earth- a horrifying image. The citizens of this era were so terrified by the thought of being ripped from their graves that many paid a high price to be buried in metal caskets. Other solutions were metal bands, called 'mort safes,' which were secured around coffins. Additionally, many early 19th century graves have tall cast iron fences surrounding the plot to deter the resurrection men. Those of less financial means simply stood vigil over the grave site until it was assumed that the corpse had decomposed enough to make it unusable. In 1832, the Anatomy Act was passed. This made grave robbing illegal. Dissection was only legally preformed upon recently executed criminals (sometimes the resurrection men themselves), or the unclaimed bodies found in poorhouses or hospitals.

the cloister, where they used to be brought and deposited in the room which they had partitioned off for the purpose and which has before been described; that the bones were afterwards thrown into the vault from the trap door; that this had been a practice for many years; and, by having the range of the Abbey, they had taken care to preserve it for themselves, by taking methods to frighten, and effectively keep away every guest that made any attempt to inhabit it." He added, moreover, "that they frequently procured bodies after word interned at or near Carlisle; and that a man, who was hanged for murder in the neighbourhood, and whose body was brought there, and hastily deposited in an obscure room, had as it was supposed, we turned to life and made it is escape; for on two men going at midnight to fetch him upon a board to the dissecting room, they found him gone, and in his place a young lady, who had sunk into a fit with terror upon their approach, and whom he believed they conveyed to a hut in the village. And some daring adventurers had lately broken in upon them; but their appearance had, as he supposed, terrified them from proceeding in their attempts; but, from the time, of the young man's being a prisoner there, and there having been pretty much alarmed, they had thought it most prudent to take away their implements till the young man was either removed or released. That he did not believe any person had ever been murdered there, though many bodies had been brought from places both near and distant, and many skeletons had been deposited in different parts of the Abbey, as well to alarm those who might see them, as to preserve them; and whenever any person came to stay there, they took care to whisper in the passages, and make other noises, to prevent their remaining in the Abbey. That he remembered hearing to one of the gentleman, he called his master, say he alarmed a lady, by coming through a trap-door into a gallery where she was walking by moon-light, though he believed she only saw his shadow.

Thus was that this great mystery at once explained, and the ghosts of Oakendale Abbey were indeed the dead; but brought thither by those unfeeling monsters of society, who make a practice of stealing our friends, and relations from the peaceful grave where their ashes, as we suppose, are deposited in rest![36]

---

[36] Like Radcliffe, Carver reveals the hauntings with rational explanations. There are no supernatural ghosts in Oakendale Abbey, no devils or demons haunt its endless halls. What makes Carver stand apart from her contemporaries is the way she uses horror. Yes, the ghosts have been rationally explained, but the reality is more terrifying than the ghosts themselves! With her inclusion of resurrection men, Carver accentuates the fact that there is no safe place in the world to hide- not even in our graves can we find peace and rest. We can still be hunted, torn from our caskets, used, abused and dissected for the pleasure of others—a horrifying thought. Carver's use of terror demonstrates that there are indeed demons in the world of men and there is no way to protect ourselves, even in the most vulnerable state of death.

The next enquiry to be made, was that of knowing by whose orders Eugene was in trapped in the Abbey; but of this the guard could give no intelligence.

Lord Oakendale questioned him very closely concerning the lady whom the man had conveyed to the hut in so alarming a state; but the guard could give no further account of her than he had already mentioned; and all that could be gathered was, that the time, in which he said it happened, corresponded exactly with that in which Laura was missing from the Abbey.

Lord Oakendale was unhappy. The thoughts of Laura, and what might be her fate, engrossed all his attention; nor was Eugene less anxious on the same score. The idea of her being confined in the Abbey with himself, filled his mind with a romantic extravagance of fancy, that they must be destined for each other.

The wild sallies of his imagination, or the more serious and pensive sentiments, which exhibited a mind formed for every noble purpose, charmed Lord Vincent; whilst Lord Oakendale viewed him with a kind of sullen hauteur, which might be well unaccounted for by the circumstances of his birth; yet, when Eugene considered him as the uncle of his Laura, a thousand attentive assiduities[37] were offered to his services; and it was with difficulty Lord Vincent could prevail upon him to accompany him back to London, in order to be

---

[37] To persist, unflagging effort

union with Eugene. Whatever might be his merits, a something, relating, no doubt, to his birth, made his mind recoil at the bare supposition; and yet Laura, with all her happiness, and all her titles, was but a wretch, if divided from her fondest hope; but she was now to engage in a new scene.

Lord Oakendale and his niece, having gratefully expressed their thanks to Mrs. Greville and all her family, for their hospitality and kindness, took their leave of the grove, and set out for London, where Lord Oakendale welcomed Laura as mistress of his house, and sole heiress to the fortunes of Oakendale. She was visited by a numerous train of company; some, who had heard her story, from real regard and friendship; others, from curiosity, and a desire of finding some flaw in her character so conspicuously superior! But her fascinating manners gained her universal admiration. She shone in the most brilliant circles, in which her eyes is continually wandered in pursuit of an object dearer to her than all the world.

It happened one evening, at an assembly, to which she went unaccompanied by Lord Oakendale, that she heard Lord Vincent announced. Her heart fluttered at the sound, and, in a moment after she beheld her loved Eugene.

He did not immediately perceive her; but the moment his eyes encountered that fair form, which his heart had ever adored, he waited not for the ceremony of a formal introduction. He made his way to her; he seized her hand, and for a few moments they forgot that the eyes of a whole assembly were riveted upon them.

Laura was covered with blushes; and some of those malignant spirits (who, envious of her charms, and the splendour in which she shone, were continually upon the watch to lower her merit) instantly took the hint, and a burst of ill-natured whispers assailed her ear. A lady, who was her chaperone, relieved her embarrassment, by making room for Eugene to sit by her, with whom she entered in to chat, as if she had been the one of his most intimate acquaintance, although she had never seen him before.

This not only made Laura feel more easy, but also gave Eugene an opportunity of uttering a thousand tender inquiries, in which his heart was truly interested. The matter of his writing to her was cleared up to the entire satisfaction of both parties, who had each lamented the silence of the other. The subject of the Abbey was but lightly touched upon. It was evident they had both been confined there at the same time; and this idea afforded sensations too tender to be discussed in their present situation.

Eugene could not withdraw himself from the side of Laura, notwithstanding she represented to him the impropriety of so particular a conduct; and it had, indeed, given occasioned for a thousand observations replete witticisms and sarcasm. "Two such strange adventurers opinion or utter a sentence. Even Lord Oakendale himself was conscience of the impropriety and disproportion between them; but the fear of seeing his niece united to Eugene would have reconciled him to yet greater disparity.

Laura avoided as much as possible all particular conversation with her uncle. She saw his health decline fast, and she could not bear the idea of giving him uneasiness. She gave up all her time to attend on him, and could seldom be prevailed on to leave him. One night she went to the Opera, where she was met by Eugene, who placed himself by her, and in any few minutes young Burlington appeared in the pit, and, without any ceremony, threw himself between them.

Laura felt herself angry, and Eugene, having gained a place on the other side of her, asked, "if he should turn the boy out of the house?" which Burlington having heard, resented with all the impetuous fury and violence of youth; and not content with abusing Eugene, in very gross terms, he called to some Oxonian's,[43] his friends, who were in the gallery, to come and give their assistance to a devilish *row* that was going to begin.

Laura grew alarmed; the eyes of the audience were turned round towards them, and several glasses in the boxes were employed to bring a nearer view of the contending parties.

---

[43] A person who has studied at Oxford University.

The lady, who came with Laura, had two daughters with her, who had never before been at an Opera; it would, therefore have been a cruel mortification to have taken them away before it was nearly half over; neither was her carriage come for her.

But Laura could not bear to be the object of wonder, and perhaps, ridicule; and she earnestly requested Eugene to get her a chair, and she would go home.

Eugene readily obeyed her command, and led her out of the pit, followed by Burlington, who expressed himself in the most childish and unhandsome terms. The truth was, he had been drinking, and dashed with liquor. The idea of being the ostensible lover of Laura, gave him airs of boyish consequence, that had disturbed the pleasure of the evening, but could not be considered in a serious light.

Eugene regarded it as no otherwise worth his notice, than as it had discomposed Laura, and deprived him sooner of her company. This he was telling her as he was going to put her into the chair, when young Burlington advanced, and seized her hand, which she drew from him with a look and expression of resentment; when just as he was about again rudely to take hold of her, one of the chairman instantly perceived, and immediately knocked him down. Eugene, without paying any regard to the circumstance, put her into the chair, and attended her to Lord Oakendale's house, in Portland-Place. He waited to see that she was perfectly recovered, and heard the following discourse from the chairman, who had knocked down young Burlington.

"Arrah, my dear young lady, I hope you will not be after being angry at my lending a blow to the lad who was after being impertinent; becase, my dear shoul, we be old acquaintance, arrah sure I cannot mistake, when I took you for an angel sent to deliver poor Patrick from pargatory; aye you're the same cratur that opened the door, and let me make my escape after I was dead, and was going to be disjointed by the hell-hounds at Oakendale; and you be too kind hearted to bring me again into trouble, seen as I would be after sarving you with my heart's blood."

Laura stared at this harangue[44] of the chairman, and after some recollection recognized, in the figure and features of this Hibernian, the very same man she had beheld in so frightful a situation in Oakendale Abbey; when, as he said, he had been hanged, and cut down before he was dead; and, having been thrown into this room, was reserved for dissection; when recovering, her opening the door released him! She was much surprised at the circumstance, to which she could not but give credit. She gave him some money, and desired he would, come again next day, when she assured him no harm should befall him; but she knew that Lord Oakendale wished to see and converse with every person that could

---

[44] A speech characterized by strong emotion.

give him any information of the transactions of the Abbey.

Patrick faithfully promised to attend in the morning, by which time Laura prepared Lord Oakendale for so extraordinary a visitor; whom when he arrived, gave the following account of himself, "That he was born at Carrick, in Ireland and at a proper age was bound apprentice to a shoemaker, with whom he nearly served his time; but getting acquainted with several bad people, he ran away from his master, and joined the White Boys,[45] with whom he committed several outrages and violent depredations, for which he was frequently afraid of being brought to justice, but good fortune always befriended him, and, after various escapes, he came to London, where he engaged in ignoble employments, and at last served in the honourable station of lamp-lighter!

"That one evening when he was lighting the lamps at Lord Oakendale's door, a female, from one of the balcony windows, accosted him and inquired his birth and education, and asked him, if he should not like to fill a more lucrative and honourable employment than that of lamp-lighter? He replied, "He was ready to undertake any business whereby he might raise his fortune, except that of committing murder, and that he could never bring himself to do;" upon which she assured him, that it was not to commit murder that she wished him to change his

---

[45] A term applied to the gangs who targeted anyone suspected of supporting the Jacobians during the French Revolution in 1794.

profession; but only to follow, and bring her an exact account of a certain young gentleman, whose abode she pointed out, and for which service he should be very handsomely rewarded.

Nothing could better suit his inclinations and his genius, than such an idle profitable business. He accordingly served her in this capacity with such indefatigable zeal, that he gave her an exact account of all the young gentleman engaged in; and, about a fortnight after this, he was sent down to Cumberland to give information to some particular persons that the above mentioned young gentleman would be in such a place, at such a time, where, he believed, he was afterwards taken and detained. That after he had undergone an examination, as to his fidelity and secrecy, he was employed to assist those wretches, and pests of society, called Resurrection men, who brought numbers of bodies to Oakendale Abbey. They were generally received in the night; and the person, who was chief superintendent, and who paid the man who procured the bodies, was named Marcel, and was brother to the woman of that nurse, who lived with Lady Oakendale, and was the same that spoke to him when he was lighting the lamp.

Patrick continued to inform his lordship that he grew tired of the employment, and thought it a shocking one; he therefore ran away, and joined a set of coiners in the neighbourhood of Penrith, where they were soon after discovered, taken, and brought to condign punishment.

At his trial he saw his old master Marcel, at the sight of whom (to use his own expression) his blood ran cold; for he supposed he was only come to watch for his condemnation, and like a crow after carrion, bespeak his body. This was really the case; for Patrick said he remembered nothing after the fatal words of condemnation had passed upon him. His mind was all in a state of confusion; and, if any thoughts did occur, they were only on the wretched state to which his body would be subjected after he was dead; nor could the clergyman, who attended him, impress any ideas of that more and more toll and immaterial part to him, which could not suffer by the hand of man.

The first idea of recollection he experienced (after the noise of the crowd and the mob that tended him to the gallows had ceased) was of extreme pain in his head and neck, and a violent oppression upon his lungs. He struggled for a few seconds, and gained respiration; a mist before his eyes seemed to vanish, and he recovered sufficient sight to perceive he was in a room with a dead body, upon one side of it. It instantly occurred to him that he was in the Abbey. He was horribly frightened, and he tried to articulate; but found his throat so swelled that he could only utter a guggling kind of sound; when in a moment the door of the room gently opened, and a beautiful creature entered, whom he supposed to be an inhabitant of that world into which he had been launched; yet, notwithstanding the appearance of this fair object, his first idea was that of making his escape which he instantly effected by passing through the door she had opened. Transient as was the glance he had of her countenance, it nevertheless made an impression never to be effaced, and the remembrance of this fair image coming to release him from a place which contained all the horrors of death, created in him a penitence for his past crimes, which would, he hoped, in some degree, atone for the commission of them.

After this he ran as fast as his legs could carry him, till night overtook his steps, and he laid down upon the grass till morning, when he asked for a crust of bread, and a draught of water, at a small cottage, from whence he begged his way up to London, where he has ever since been in honest employment, and has sincerely and truly repented of his past crimes. When he saw Laura handed out of the opera house by Eugene, he instantly remembered them both; and the strong propensity he had to speak to her got the better of all decorum.

Thus ended the narrative of Patrick O'Dennis, at which Lord Oakendale expressed much surprise. He handsomely rewarded Patrick for his trouble, and strongly recommended to him to persevere in his good resolutions.

Lord Oakendale made some comments upon Patrick's narrative, and seeming to be in very good humour, Laura took occasioned to mention the circumstances of the preceding night, not omitting to enlarge upon the firm and polite conduct of Eugene, in opposition to that of the more boyish and insolent behaviour of Mr. Burlington. Lord Oakendale could not but admit and approve of the former; and Laura gained so far upon his good temper, as to obtain leave to dismiss that young fop from any love-like pretensions towards her. This was a great step gained, and Laura promised, in her turn, to make some concessions equally pleasing to her uncle.

Comfort seemed once more to dawn upon her, and she had sometimes (though not often) the happiness of meeting Eugene. Lord Vincent frequently pressed him to make another choice, since there was no probability of Lord Oakendale's giving his consent to an union with Laura, and to see Eugene settled in marriage, was the first wish of his father. But although Eugene received all the advances from the Misses, and all the overtures from their mothers and aunts, which are authorized and encouraged by the present race of females, yet was his heart faithful to its first attachment; and, however he might despair of gaining Laura, he could never allow the idea of another woman as the sole object of his affections. Indeed, these firm resolutions were become highly necessary; for a young widow of the name of Sackville, laid such a well-regulated siege to the heart of Eugene, and had so many, and such fascinating charms, that it was almost impossible to resist her power. She was besides highly favoured, and strongly recommended by Lord Vincent, for his future daughters; and this being the case, Eugene was more frequently thrown into her company than he would otherwise have wished; consequently the world had pronounced them a pair destined for each other, with the addition of the most violent love subsisting between them.

The report could not fail to reach the ears of Laura. She did not at first give the smallest credit to it, but only considered it as the idle story of the day. It was, however, so frequently, and so strongly repeated, that a spark of jealousy began to light up in her mind, and several little circumstances kindled the flame to a tormenting state of uneasiness and suspense.

She seldom saw Eugene. He never came to lord Oakendale's; and the ill state of his lordship's health confined her very much at home. Whenever she had met Eugene he was in company with Mrs. Sackville. Her heart could not easily give credit to his infidelity, yet a thousand corroding fears rendered her miserable.

During this state of uncertainty Lord Oakendale grew every day more debilitated, and his health declined very fast. Laura was his sole comfort, and to her he looked for every satisfaction the world could give him. He had observed her late uneasiness, and, perhaps, guessed the cause, in which he could not but rejoice, however he might feel hurt at the effect. He redoubled his kindness to her; he told her she would be sole mistress of all his wealth at his decease, and often signified how ardently he wished her to divide it with some worthy man.

What were wealth and honours to Laura! There was, indeed, an object dearer to her than all the world; and that object was now said to be devoted to another. How cruel was her fate! yet a more severe one awaited her.[46]

Her uncle grew every day worse; his disorder was slow but of such a nature as no remedy could reach. He found he must soon pay the debt of nature, and a lowness of spirit seized him. Something seemed to press upon his mind with a particular weight of uneasiness. Laura, ever attentive, and willing to mitigate (as far as was in her power) the sorrow that seemed to oppress him, used every method she could devise to remove the melancholy he laboured under, at the same time that her own mind was cruelly agitated.

Lord Oakendale seemed sensible of her kindness. He would gaze at her for hours together, whilst he uttered the most bitter size; and the pain of his mind seemed to increase the malady of his body, and hastened his dissolution. It was in one of these moments that Laura said, "Is there anything I can do that will make my dear uncle more easy and composed?"

---

[46] Though it may seem insignificant at first glance, this moment is an excellent example of Carver's use of creating extreme anxiety for her readers. We are only a few pages from the end of the novel and we are expecting closure; however, Carver's use of narrative structure and language never allows us to feel secure or rested for a moment. A more severe fate awaits Laura? What could possible by next? Hasn't she been through enough? Carver focuses more on separation anxiety and dread, rather than accentuating happy endings.

"There is," replied Lord Oakendale; "but will my Laura make the sacrifice? I know it is a weakness in me to desire it; but it is a weakness I have tried in vain to conquer, and my peace depends upon her word."

"Speak," said Laura, in an agitated voice, though far from suspecting the nature of the request, "and be assured of all in my power."

"Can you, then," said Lord Oakendale "will my Laura promise, sacredly promise, never to marry Eugene Vincent?"

"Stop," said Laura; "Oh! save me from this conflict." Lord Oakendale sat with eagerness, and death depicted on his countenance. He seemed impatiently waiting for a reply; yet trembling lest he had made a request which could not be granted; at the same time fearing that his weak the frame could not support a refusal.

"Alas!" said Laura (turning her head this way and that way, in the most distracted state of terror and perplexity) have I no friend to advise me in this cruel conflict? Oh! my lord, Eugene is dearer to me than—" here she stopped, and a violent burst of tears, in some degree, relieved her.

During this time lord Oakendale trembled, and appeared convulsed. He grasped the hand of Laura, and faintly pronounced, "I am dying!" She was extremely terrified; and, as she supported him with one arm, she rang the bell with the other for assistance. He was conveyed to bed, and proper advice was immediately sent for.

The state of Laura was very little better than that of her uncle. She had not as yet given the fatal promise that would seal her misery; but the dying situation of Lord Oakendale, and the wish he had so devoutly expressed, seemed to require it. She went to his chamber fully determined to make the sacrifice of her happiness, if it was necessary to his peace of mind.

As she proceeded to Lord Oakendale's room she reflected on the consequence of what she was about to do. What were riches, honours, titles, fame, or any worldly comfort, without the charming liberty of bestowing them on the only object of her love! Yet, might not the promise she was about to make be of the utmost consequence to herself, as seemed so necessary to calm the despairing spirit of Lord Oakendale; that promise, which to confirm, tore her heart asunder. In what estimation might it be held by the person for whose sake alone and she would withhold it. Ah! (but there was madness in that thought) it might be a happy release to Eugene, and at once enable him to cancel those vows which had made her so binding. These reflections brought her to the chamber-door; and, upon her entering, the physicians informed her Lord Oakendale had but a few minutes to live, and that he had never once spoken since she left him!

She approached the bed; she took his hand, and kneeling down, she pressed it to her lips, where the tears fell in large drops from her eyes. He looked at her with the tenderest pity. She thought him perfectly sensible; and she was going to pronounce her promise, when he fixed his hand (already clammy with the dew of death) upon her lips, as if to prevent her speaking. She raised up her eyes in tenderest expression to Heaven for the release; and, although he mourned, perhaps, inwardly, his countenance conveyed content and approbation. For a few seconds he appeared struggling for speech. He withdrew his hands from Laura's, and, joining them in a supplication form, he articulated "Bless my niece!" and expired.

Laura was extremely shocked at the sudden approach of his death, and she grieved for him with the most affectionate sincerity. She was perfectly satisfied that he wished to recall the promise he had desired her to make, and was convinced that the hand of death had awakened him to contrition, and a proper sense of the cruelty his more lively feelings would have imposed.

Laura found herself in possession of all his vast fortune; and she had the comfort and advice of her dear Madame du Frene in the arrangement of the funeral, and other necessary matters. She had likewise the satisfaction of asking that dear friend concerning Eugene, to whom Madame du Frene had always been extremely partial. Lord Oakendale had on that account not shewn her so much favour as he would otherwise have done; and during his illness Laura had been but little able to meet with her.

When she asked concerning him, Madame du Frene looked grave, and only be replied "he was well."

Laura did not feel contented with the answer; but a certain dislike to lead to the subject, unless more encouraged by her friend, prevented her adding more at present. She thought it unkind that Eugene never made any inquiries after her; and, as she did not yet go into public, she never chanced to see him. Soon after, however, she returned her visits, and appeared in public. Her sabled dress diminished nothing of her beauty, and the knowledge of her large and independent fortune gave additional charms to her person. She once or twice saw Eugene, and was shocked at the coldness of his address and manners towards her. He always looked uncommonly grave, and avoided any further conversation than the common-place forms of ceremony required. Such behaviour was to her unaccountable, and cruel in the extreme. He could, she thought, but have behaved in this matter had she really made that promise to Lord Oakendale, which she had considered as so fatal to her peace.

Harassed and fretted as she was from this conduct, and finding neither riches or admiration afforded her the smallest happiness in this uncertain state, she determined to come to a more particular explanation with Madame du Frene on the subject so near her heart.

She accordingly took the opportunity of expressing her surprise and wonder at the coldness of Eugene's behaviour.

Madame du Frene remained silent for some moments, and then said, "My dear Laura, how often, in your days of childhood, have I endeavoured to prepare your mind for those disappointments which come nearest the heart, and which, if borne with pious resignation, are the brightest ornaments to the christian character. I am truly sorry to have occasion now to enforce this doctrine; but Eugene is, I am informed, engaged to marry Mrs. Sackville." Here she stopped, and Laura sat with her arms rested on a table, and her hands covered her face. She sighed bitterly, and when she looked up, Madame du Frene had the mortification to observe marks of the most extreme sorrow depicted in her countenance.

Nothing more passed at the present time. Madame du Frene was so much hurt at the appearance of woe which Laura's looks expressed, that she was resolved to speak to Eugene upon the subject, although she had little or no hopes of ever seeing them united.

It happened soon after that Madame was, by her own contrivance, thrown into company with Eugene; when she purposely introduced the subject of Laura, observing upon her immense fortune, and still greater merits;

adding her earnest hopes, that she would bestow it upon some man truly worthy of so rich a blessing.

Eugene sighed, and asked (in a melancholy tone) "If Laura was likely to be married?"

"Not that I know," replied Madame du Frene, "I should imagine she would be extremely careful how she formed a second attachment, having been so cruelly disappointed in her first."

Eugene seemed much agitated, and, after a pause said, "if she had suffered any disappointment, it was of her own inflicting; and the cruelty was deeply and forever transfixed in the bosom of another."

Madame du Frene replied, "Good God! what is it you mean? When nature formed the fairest of its compositions, no material was omitted; and Laura is, I am certain of that disposition, as would rather suffer pain herself then inflict it upon others."

"Why then," said Eugene, "did she make that rash—I will say it that accursed promise?"

"What promise!" replied Madame du Frene; "she never did make any; Lord Oakendale was taken speechless before she had time to pronounce a promise, which nothing but the agonies of death would have exhorted from her; and even in that moment she wavered, and professed that you were dear to her than life! Nay," continued Madame du Frene, "she had the satisfaction of knowing, and being assured, that her uncle approved of her conduct, and blessed her with his parting breath!"

Thus was this distressing business brought to an amicable conclusion; and Madame du Frene had the inexpressible felicity of reconciling two lovers whose hearts had never been divided.

It appeared that Lord Oakendale, extremely desirous to break the bonds which so closely united Eugene and Laura, had mentioned to some particular friends that Laura had given him a solemn promise never to marry Eugene. In consequence of this report Lord Vincent's pride took the alarm, and he repeated it to Eugene with exaggerated proofs.

Thus had these two unhappy men nearly destroyed the felicity of those most dear to them by their ill judging zeal, and still more blameable subversion of the truth.

Eugene, with a mind distracted with disappointment, flew to dissipation to dispel his misery; and, falling in the way of a young and fascinating widow, he had nearly formed that contract with her, which his honor would have obliged him to such; and nothing but death could have dissolved.

The death of Lord Vincent, soon after these occurrences, gave to his son, titles, wealth and power. His intentions had long been fixed, and the merits of Laura were amply rewarded by an union with her lover Eugene. Some of their summers were passed in

Cumberland; and the virtues of Lord Vincent and Laura
soon dispelled

THE HORRORS OF OAKENDALE ABBEY.[47]

-FINIS-

---

[47] Carver's romantic theme in the book is not a typical love story.
Rather than focusing on the healing power of love and the reunion of
lovers, Carver exploits the terror found in separation anxiety. Even as
her novel draws to a close, it is only in two brief and underdeveloped
sentences that we discover the lovers reunited. In Carver's world, terror
and anxiety supersedes happy endings.

For Further Reading:

Auerbach, Nina. *Woman and the Demon: The Life of a Victorian Myth.* Cambridge:Harvard Press, 1982. (Any of Auerbach's books make for wonderfully insightful reading.)

Clemens, Valdine. *The Return of the Repressed: Gothic Horror from The Castle of Otranto to Alien.* New York: State University Press, 1999.

Ellis, Kate Ferguson. *The Contested Castle: Gothic Novels and the Subversion of Domestic Ideology.*Chicago: University of Illinois, 1989.

Estes, Clarissa Pinkola. *Women Who Run With the Wolves: Myths and Stories of the Wild Woman Archetype.* New York: Ballantine, 1995.

Jung, C. G. *The Archetypes and the Collective Unconscious.* Trans. R. F. C. Hull. Princeton: Princeton University Press, 1990.

Von Franz, Marie-Louise. *Shadow and Evil in Fairy Tales.* Boston: Shambhala, 1995.

Warner, Marina. *From the Beast to the Blonde: On Fairy Tales and Their Tellers.* New York: Farrar, Straus and Giroux, 1995. (This is a wonderfully useful book—I find myself referring to it again and again, for it does what all great books do- inspires the reader to want to learn more...while you're at it- read anything by Marina Warner—She fills you with ideas and wonderful insight.)

Other books by
ZITTAW PRESS

BUNGAY CASTLE
Elizabeth Bonhote
Edited by Curt Herr

THE ABBESS
William-Henry Ireland
Edited by Jeffrey Kahan

HAUNTED PRIORY
Stephen Cullen
Edited by Franz J. Potter

LaVergne, TN USA
16 September 2010

197256LV00001B/95/A